Buck Innes was about to saddle his horse when he saw the men coming from the mouth of Shotgun Canyon. There were three of them. On horseback. With rifles. Just as Buck yanked the Colt Peacemaker out of its holster, the first shot was fired. Buck hit the ground so hard he tasted dirt. Two more shots pinged off the ground near Buck's legs.

Well, hell, he muttered to himself, what're you going to do, just lie here and let them kill you? Shoot. Shoot as fast as you can. Make them pay.

Jumping to his feet he began firing, holding the trigger back and fanning the hammer with his left hand until the firing pin hit an empty shell. Then he turned and ran, heading for the thick buck brush. A bullet tugged at his shirttail. Another knocked his hat off. He knew he was as good as dead.

The three men, whoever they were, had what they wanted: Spooky's lost gold mine. And it looked to Buck like it wouldn't be more'n a few moments before there'd be nobody left alive to say it wasn't theirs.

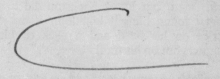

DOYLE TRENT
SHOTGUN CANYON

ZEBRA BOOKS
KENSINGTON PUBLISHING CORP.

ZEBRA BOOKS

are published by

Kensington Publishing Corp.
475 Park Avenue South
New York, NY 10016

First printing: November, 1990

Printed in the United States of America

Chapter One

Something about this young woman walking up the path to the boarding house made Buck Innes uncomfortable. It made him squirm in his chair, take his boots off the porch railing and sit up straight.

She had trouble. He could tell by the pinched look on her face. And there was something else, something dimly familiar about her. It gnawed at his memory, bringing a frown to his own leathery face.

He first saw her the day before at the railroad depot. Now that he'd been forced into retirement and had nothing else to do, he sometimes hauled his bones over to the depot to watch the train come in and see who got off. It was interesting. Just about every kind of human animal a man would want to see came to Cripple Creek. Most of them got on a train at Denver or Colorado Springs, then transferred to the narrow gauge Florence and Cripple Creek Railroad. After climbing five thousand feet and traveling through Phantom Canyon where the railroad seemed to hang onto the side of a cliff, they were ready to get off.

Among them were the rich mine owners and bankers in fine wool coats and vests. They all had gold watch chains draped across their well-fed bellies. There were smooth-faced lawyers, gold brokers and politicians in high beaver hats. There were ladies in fine linen clothes with lacy feathery hats pinned to their heads. And the working stiffs. More and more hard rock miners in baggy clothes were coming from the played out mines in Utah and Nevada, looking for a job. Then there were the gamblers in pointy shoes and the whores overloaded with cheap perfume who came to Cripple Creek to mine the miners.

This one didn't fit any of those categories. She was dressed in a plain gray traveling suit with mutton chop shoulders, a flared skirt that came to her ankles and a cloth belt that pulled it all in at the middle. She was slender, with short blond hair and a pillbox hat on her head. Pretty. Not Upper Ten but not laboring class either. More like a store clerk or a bank teller.

Something about her reminded Buck of someone, but at the time he couldn't figure out who.

When she stepped out of the little narrow Pullman car carrying a tin suitcase, she hesitated as if she wasn't sure she wanted to be there. Cripple Creek must have been a whole new world to her. It sat in a huge volcanic bowl at an altitude of over nine thousand five hundred feet. The air was cool even in August. From the top of the bowl a man could see Pikes Peak in one direction and the Sangre de Cristo mountains in another. The depot was always busy, and nearby Bennett Avenue was always loaded with horse-drawn traffic and pedestrians. Mine dumps of fractured rock, and tall mine headframes surrounded the town.

Buck had watched idly as she approached a ticket

window and said something to the agent, a man Buck knew as Oldham. The agent squinted from under his green eyeshade and pointed toward Bennett Avenue. Buck watched as she left, carrying her suitcase. For a long moment he tried to recall where he'd seen her before, then decided she only looked like someone he'd known somewhere.

Now, as she walked up the path to Mrs. Davenport's boarding house, he had a gut-deep suspicion she was coming to see him — and wasn't bringing good news.

"Mornin', Miss," he said when she was at the porch steps. She obviously wasn't used to the altitude and had to catch her breath before she could speak. "Purty day," Buck said, trying to be pleasant.

"Sir, could you tell me . . . I've been told that I could find Mr. Buck Innes here."

He unfolded his lean six-foot frame from the chair and pushed back his hat. A sheaf of gray hair fell across his forehead. Trying to keep the apprehension out of his voice, he said, "I'm Buck."

"I, uh, sir, I've been told that you know my father."

And then it came to him. He should have known. "Are you . . . ?" He squinted at her, trying to see the resemblance.

"I am Anita Hallows." She had to look up to him from the end of the path at the bottom of the steps. "My father is Andrew Hallows."

In spite of the uncomfortable feeling she gave him, he had to grin. "Little Annie? I wouldn't of knowed you. Don't you remember me, Annie?"

She smiled. It was a weak weary smile. "Yes, sir, I do, but only vaguely. I remember a Mr. Innes who was a friend of my parents. I'm trying to locate my father. No one seems to know where he is."

7

"Well, come up here and set down and get your wind, Annie. Or should I call you Miss Hallows now?"

Later, when he was thinking about it, he knew he shouldn't have been surprised. He'd been worried about old Spooky Hallows. In fact, he'd said just a few days ago that he wondered what had become of him. Buck and an old miner named Hadigan were sitting on the porch with their boots parked on the porch railing when he'd mentioned it.

"Ain't seen or heard of him for three-four weeks now," Hadigan had said. "Somebody ought to go look for 'im."

Buck was the most likely to go looking for Spooky Hallows. He knew him better than anyone else. He knew Andy "Spooky" Hallows long before gold was found at Cripple Creek, back when it was cattle that made everyone a living in this territory.

Folks started calling Andy Hallows "Spooky" a year ago last spring after he got to coming and going in the night. Soon everyone, even Buck and others who'd known him for many years, were calling him by that name. No one knew where he came from or where he went. A lot of men wanted to know. A lot of men had tried to follow him. They got no farther than the cemetery on the other side of town. Old Spooky and his two burros had always disappeared in the brush and timber west of there.

Buck never tried to follow him. Where Andy went was his business and none of Buck Innes's. Besides, Buck didn't want to give up his comforts at the boarding house. But he was beginning to worry.

Now his daughter had shown up. Looking at her again, he could see the small-boned face of Mrs. Hallows and Spooky's pale blue eyes. Buck hadn't seen Anita Hallows since she was a little tow-headed tyke running around in a hand-me-down dress two sizes too big for her. Her dresses were all given to her by cousins, and were cut off at the bottom. The sleeves had to be rolled up to free her small dirty hands.

He got her seated in the chair next to his, the one Hadigan had just vacated not ten minutes earlier. She sat primly, knees together, hands folding and unfolding in her lap. Buck's mind registered the fact that she wore no wedding ring, only a silver band on the longest finger, the kind of ring that cost only three or four day's pay. The little pillbox hat had been tilted by a breeze from the west, and now she straightened it with nervous hands. His first impression of her was correct. Her slightly crooked nose kept her from being a classic beauty, but she was attractive. She had a firm chin, full soft lips, and the fair skin and delicate features he remembered in Andy's wife. Only her eyes reminded him of her father. The eyes were weathered a little, faded, kind of tight at the corners. He reckoned she hadn't exactly lived a life of luxury.

"Where'd you come from, Miss Hallows? You sure have grown up. How long has it been, twenty years? Twenty-two?"

"I . . . I don't remember when I saw you last, Mr. Innes. I can barely remember my father."

"Yeah, I recall your mother takin' you away when you was . . . you must of been about three years old. Maybe four."

"Yes. Mother died two years ago. I wrote my father about it. He always sent us money, but he never wrote anything. I hope he received my letter."

"Danged if I know. He didn't mention it. But Old Spooky, er, Andy, ain't been very talkative lately. He comes and goes without hardly talkin' to anybody."

"I'm very much concerned about him, Mr. Innes. He has always sent us money regularly, but I have received nothing for over a month now. It's not the money. It's, well, he's the only parent I have left, and I have always felt guilty about not coming to see him. I never was really sure he would want to see me."

"Well . . ." Buck wanted to lean back and park his boots on the porch railing, but that probably wouldn't be gentlemanly. "I can't speak for Andy, but if he was sendin' you money he must, uh . . ." He didn't know how to finish what he had in mind to say.

"Anyway, I would like very much to find him. Do you happen to know where he goes? I've been told that he just appears and disappears."

"Yep, he's struck 'er rich up there beyond Signal Peak somewheres, and he ain't tellin' where. He never filed a claim 'cuz he'd have to write down the location, and he ain't about to give away the location."

"Is that where the money came from? He never wrote anything, just addressed an envelope, put some paper money in it and mailed it. Most of the time from Cripple Creek and once from Florissant."

"He's got a good 'un up there. Every week he comes down in the dark and parks his two donkeys in a pen at his cabin, and next mornin' takes two donkey loads of high grade ore to the mill. I heard some of that ore assayed out at more'n six hundred dollars a ton."

"Is that good?"

"That makes his mine the best one around, and there's some rich ones around here."

"When was the last time you you saw him?"

Buck scratched his jaw, realized he hadn't shaved

for two days, and wished he were more presentable. "I was just tryin' to remember the other day. Old Hadigan and I was talkin' about him. I think it was at least three weeks ago, and then he was across the street where all I could do was wave at him. I heard he'd just taken some more high grade stuff to the mill."

"Are you still friends?"

"Oh, yeah. I never had no quarrel with Andy, and as far as I know he never had no quarrel with me. He just ain't been very talkative lately."

"Are you friends enough to look for him?" The pale blue eyes were squinting a little now and fixed on Buck's gray ones.

There it was. She had worries and wanted his help. That's what had made him uncomfortable. He liked the kind of life he was living now, and riding off into those mountains looking for someone without a clue as to where to look wasn't the way he wanted to spend his time. He squirmed in his wooden chair, the chair with a thick cushion on it.

He'd needed a cushion ever since the bank holdup.

"Well, uh, I don't know. Old Spooky don't want nobody pokin' around in his business, and he's been known to take a shot at men that tried to follow him. He'll show up one of these days. Or one of these nights."

"Oh." Disappointment clouded her face as she looked away. Buck was trying to figure out what to say next when she spoke again: "I went to his cabin last evening. A gentleman at the hotel told me where it is. The door had been broken open, and it looked as though no one had been in it for some time."

"Is that so?" Buck sat up a little straighter. It relieved the ache in his right hip. "You sure about that?"

11

✗ "I'm sure the door was broken. There was a big padlock, but the latch was torn completely off and the door was partially open."

"Dang. Somebody busted in. Did you tell the deputy about it?"

"I couldn't find him. He wasn't in his office."

"He ain't never in. I don't know what he does to earn his keep." Buck was about to volunteer to go over to Spooky's cabin and have a look when the front door opened and Hadigan came out.

"Oh, excuse me," the old miner said. "I didn't know you had company."

Twisting in his chair, Buck said, "You'd never guess who this young lady is, Hadigan."

"No," Hadigan said, trying to study the girl's face without looking directly at her. "No, couldn't guess in a million years." He stood in his slouchy bib overalls and jackboots. A floppy wide-brim hat was tilted to one side on his head. He shaved only once a week, and tomorrow was his day to shave.

"We was just talkin' about Spooky Hallows," Buck said, "when who come along but his daughter. This here is Anita Hallows."

"No." Hadigan's jaw dropped open and he studied her face without embarrassment now. "I didn't know he had a daughter. He never said nothin' about it."

"I knowed, but I almost forgot. Ain't seen her since she was a little bitty thing." Then Buck remembered his manners and introduced the two. "This is Hadigan, Miss Hallows. He was smarter than most miners. He sold his claim for enough to quit diggin' and retire."

"How do you do, Mr. Hadigan. Do you know my father?"

"Sure. Ever'body knows 'im. Know 'im when they see 'im, that is. I spoke to 'im a few times is all."

12

"Then you have no idea where he is?"

"No, 'fraid I don't. Like Buck said, me and him was just talkin' about that."

"Do you think something could have happened to him? I mean, if he's wandering alone up there in the mountains, something could have happened."

"There's always that chance," Buck answered. "A man can break a leg or . . ." He shut up before he could tell about the men who wanted to find Spooky's mine, and what some men would do if they did find it.

"I suppose I could get the sheriff to go and look for him."

"Won't do no good," Hadigan said. "Lots of men have looked for 'im, and never found 'im. And that deputy ain't about to go runnin' off in all directions without some idea where he's goin'."

"Oh my." The young woman's features pulled together in a tight knot. She bit her lower lip. Buck wanted to say something that would make her feel better.

"Aw, he'll show up. He always does." He said it but he wasn't sure it was the truth.

"But with his cabin being broken into and all, I'm worried. Even though I haven't seen him for many years, he is my father."

The two men didn't know what to say so they said nothing.

"Do you suppose, Mr. Innes, that you could find him?"

Buck was hesitant, but Hadigan wasn't. "If anybody can find 'im, old Buck can. He knows them mountains like he knows this porch, don't you Buck."

"Naw. There's a lot of territory up there that no man has seen. No white man. None that ever came back, anyway. We lost cattle up there that we never did find."

"Then my father might never be found." She wiped a tear out of her left eye with the palm of her hand.

It was true, and Buck knew it but he didn't want to say it. The girl stood, weary, shoulders slumped. She looked to Buck like a spanked puppy. He couldn't stand it.

"Tell you what, Miss Hallows, I'll go over to Spooky's cabin with you and look around. Maybe we'll find a clue or somethin'. You never know, old Spooky might've come back." Buck stood and pulled his gray, wide-brim hat down to his eyebrows.

"I would surely appreciate that, Mr. Innes."

To Hadigan, Buck said, "Tell Mrs. Davenport I'll be late for dinner and ask her to save me somethin'."

Chapter Two

Walking was easier now that Buck had exchanged his high-heeled riding boots for flat-heeled jackboots, the kind the miners wore. He didn't need riding boots anymore. Riding horses was something he'd done little of since the bank robbery. When he thought about it he had to snort up his sleeve. Most of his life he'd ridden horses. He wouldn't have walked fifty feet when there was a horse available. And there was always a horse available. He'd tried. He really wanted to. But a day on a horse had the old bullet wound yelping with pain.

The girl was sensibly shod in button up high-top shoes. She followed him silently down the narrow path through the tall grass and yellow wild flowers to Bennett Avenue. At Bennett, they had to stop to let a string of four heavy wagons loaded with ore go past. Each wagon was pulled by six horses. The street was dry and the wagons raised dust. A buggy with a canopy pulled by two high-stepping bay horses went by in the opposite direction. Traffic was heavy on the plank sidewalk too. Miners in dirty, baggy clothes stepped aside for the ladies in fine long dresses. Well-dressed gentlemen tipped their hats at the ladies. The ladies all carried parasols to keep the high country sun from darkening their complexions. Buck and Anita Hallows waited beneath a canvas awning attached to a pine board building until they saw a chance to cross the street.

When the traffic cleared, Buck and Anita Hallows hurried across Bennett and followed a rocky road to Meyers Avenue. At Meyers, Buck looked straight ahead, hoping Miss Hallows wouldn't notice the cribs where the oldest of the whores plied their trade. Farther up the street the whores weren't whores but Ladies of the Evening, and they lived in brick houses with elegant furnishings. That's where the High Tenners went when they could get away from their wives. The mine workers, the single ones, had to be content with the cribs. Once across Meyers, Buck and the young woman took a footpath south through the tall grass, rocks and bushy cinquefoil. Spooky Hallows's one-room log cabin was four blocks south on the edge of a rocky gulch. A pole fence surrounded it and three acres of mountain grass and wildflowers of every color. The wooden gate in the fence was open. That alone was proof that Spooky wasn't at home. He kept his burros inside the fence when he was there.

The girl stayed behind Buck as he approached the cabin door. Sure enough, it was busted. The hasp had been torn completely off. Someone had used a crowbar on it. The plank door was half-open. Hollering a greeting and waiting for an invitation to come in would have been useless, and Buck stepped through the door. He'd been there before. He and Spooky had shared some elk steaks and a bottle of whiskey in that cabin. They'd played checkers and

16

swapped stories about the old days. They both liked to recall the years before some cowboy found gold on Poverty Gulch, before there was a town here, back when everyone in these parts did their trading at the town of Florissant. They'd been neighbors then. The Innes family had four homesteads and about five hundred cattle grazing on the public domain. Andy had only his one homestead and about a hundred and fifty cattle, but he kept his wife and baby well fed by hunting and trapping.

Nothing in the cabin had changed. The wooden bunk covered with ragged blankets was still there, and so were the home-made table and two chairs. The cast iron two-lid cook stove, the home-made shelf holding what looked like the same sack of Arbuckles and the same sacks of sugar, flour and the like were all there. Even the same ragged mackinaw hung from a nail on a wall. Buck stepped inside, his boots clomping on the wooden floor. The shallow lid from an empty lard can was still on the table, full of cigarette butts. Spooky had taken to those Duke ready-rolled cigarettes just last year. Stepping farther into the room, Buck let his eyes rove over everything.

Uh-oh. The steamer trunk against the north wall, the one that had always been locked, was open. The hasp had been pried off.

The girl was standing in the doorway when Buck turned to her. "Is this the way you found it, Miss Hallows?"

"Yes." She was wide-eyed and looked to be ready to bolt and run.

"That trunk over there. Andy always kept it locked. Have you looked in it?"

"No, I . . . I was a little scared."

"Nothin' to be scared of now. Take a look and see

what's inside."

"Would you mind looking Mr. Innes?" She stayed in the doorway.

"Well, I, it's prob'ly got some personal stuff in it. Family stuff that's none of my business. You're his daughter so go ahead and see what you can see. There's nothin' to be scared of."

Moving cautiously, like she was afraid something alive would jump out of the trunk, Anita Hallows knelt before it and looked inside. Buck stood behind her and looked over her shoulder. There were papers in no kind of order, and a satin pillow with a gold-colored fringe on the edges. The words "St. Louis" were printed on it in gold letters. A souvenir from back east, maybe. There were a few old faded pictures, one showing a smiling young man, a woman and a small child. The picture was so faded the faces weren't recognizable, but at the bottom someone had written in ink: Lottie. Anita. Andrew.

Anita Hallows studied the picture a moment before she put it aside. No longer fearful, she dug through the papers to the bottom of the trunk. She found a few china dishes of fine quality, some lacy handkerchiefs and old letters, so old the paper was crumbling. All keepsakes. There were more old pictures, some baby clothes carefully folded, a pair of tiny slippers and a baby's nursing bottle. More keepsakes. She pulled out a paper with her mother's name and address written on it. And then she found the letter she had written to her father telling about her mother's death.

Looking up at Buck, she said, "Well, he got my letter. Apparently he didn't care."

He wanted to ask if her mother had cared about Andy, and why she had left him anyway, but he didn't. It was none of his business. Clearing his throat, he asked, "He did keep on sendin' money, you said?"

"Yes." She stood, looking down at the trunk. "There's nothing in there about the location of his mine, is there?"

"Naw. He wouldn't put it down on paper."

"Well," she turned to face him, "suppose something happened to him, how would his heirs know where to find his treasure?"

"I reckon he never thought about that. But don't go convincin' yourself that somethin' happened to him. Uh, you said heirs, you're the next of kin, ain't you?"

"Yes, now that mother has gone. I don't think he had any brothers or sisters, but even if he did I would obviously inherit everything."

"I reckon."

"Oh, I wish he'd filed a claim. Or something." She turned back to the trunk, studied it a moment, then faced Buck again. "Do you think anyone will ever find his mine?"

"Sure. Somebody'll find it. There's prospectors all over this country. Somebody'll find it sooner or later. If I was Andy, I'd sure file a claim."

"What would you do if you found it, Mr. Innes?"

"Me? I'd talk Andy into claimin' it legal. If I found it, somebody else could."

"You wouldn't claim it for yourself?"

"Naw. Not if it was Andy's."

"You were really good friends, weren't you?"

"As good a friends as there is. Ain't seen much of him lately, but far as I'm concerned we're still good friends."

"I would like to hire you to look for him."

19

"Hire me?"

"Yes. I don't have much money, but I can pay you a little. Do you think it will take very long?"

"Well now, I don't know. I ain't gonna go trampin' around in those hills just because Andy ain't showed up lately. Besides, I don't get around as good as I used to."

"I've been told that you know those hills better than anyone else."

"Prob'ly do, but that don't mean I could find your daddy."

She turned slowly, head down and walked outside. He followed her out, closed the door, tried to fix the broken hasp, and when he couldn't, left the door slightly ajar. Near the door was a pile of shattered rocks that wasn't there the last time Buck had visited Spooky. Looked like gold ore that Spooky had planned to haul to the mill. Buck could see that the grass in the little trap of a pasture hadn't been grazed on for some time. The burro droppings were old and dry. Spooky Hallows and his burros were missing, no doubt about that.

When he caught up with Anita Hallows her eyes were moist, and she wiped them with the palms of her hands. Sniffing, she spoke in a tight voice, "I'm so worried. He is my father. I would give anything to find him."

"Well, like I said, Miss Hallows, he could show up anytime."

Her voice suddenly contained a hint of anger. "What am I supposed to do? Just wait and worry?"

"Well, uh . . ." He didn't know what else to say. She walked on up the path through the rocks and grass. Now he was following her. At Bennett Avenue, she stopped. "I'm staying at the Palace Hotel. I'll stay a few days and . . . and pray."

"I sure hope he's all right, Miss Hallows. I'm bettin' he is."

But as Buck Innes walked back up the path to Mrs. Davenport's boarding house, he admitted to himself that he'd lied. Right then he wouldn't have bet a nickel that Spooky Hallows was still alive.

Chapter Three

Mrs. Davenport groused at him for being late, but she had kept an iron pot of boiled beef, spuds and turnips on the stove for him. He washed his face out of a tin pan on the back porch, dried himself on a towel made of a flour sack, ran his fingers through his gray hair and parked himself at the kitchen table. While he sat with his fingers drumming the red-and-white-checkered table cloth, she took a chipped china plate from her cupboard and ladled it full. Then she opened a tin bread box on a shelf, took out a half-loaf of homemade bread and set that on the table. Next came some butter and plum preserves. Finally, she poured coffee out of a galvanized coffee pot.

"Thank you kindly, ma'am," Buck said as he began stuffing his face.

Mrs. Davenport didn't know it, but while he was eating he was watching the way her plump rump moved inside the shapeless cotton dress. He was trying to visualize how she'd look without the dress. Mrs. Davenport was the widow of Bert Davenport who took his last ride in a mine skip when the hoist brakes let go and dropped it two hundred feet. He'd left her a three-bedroom clapboard house, and she earned her living by taking in boarders. Right now she had only Buck and Hadigan, but there was room for more if Buck and Hadigan would share their rooms. Buck wouldn't.

Watching her, Buck Innes again speculated on how she'd be in bed, and wondered if he could get her there. He was gonna try. One of these days he was gonna pat her on the rump and proposition her. If she got mad he'd apologize all over the place, but maybe she wouldn't get mad.

It had worked before. Buck had never married and he had a reputation at times as a womanizer. Back before gold was found, there was always a Saturday night dance in one of the ranch houses, and although the men outnumbered the women six or eight to one, Buck got his share of the single ones under the blankets. At first, when he was a teenager, he was shy around the girls and didn't know what to say to them. That changed when an older woman talked him outside one Saturday night. They'd no more than got out of the lamplight from the windows when she grabbed him by the crotch of his pants and pulled him into the back of a wagon.

He was shy no more.

From then on, when he saw an unattached woman who looked likely, he wasted no words. Most of the time it didn't work, but sometimes it did. Of course there were drawbacks to that approach. Buck got into more than his share of fistfights. One jealous cowboy he'd knocked down went out to his horse and came back with a hogleg pistol. Buck didn't think it was possible for a man to outrun bullets, but he sure did it that night. Another drawback—and Buck couldn't help feeling a little sad when he thought about it — was the nice girls would have nothing to do with him. The older he got the more he regretted that. Thinking back, he could remember several girls he would liked to have trotted in double harness with. He envied the men who'd treated them right and married them.

"Mr. Innes." His landlady was seated across the table from him now. "A gentleman came to the door today looking for a place to stay. I don't suppose you would reconsider and share your room."

"No ma'am," he answered around a mouthful of beef. "A man has a right to some privacy, and I ain't sharin' my room." He considered saying something like maybe he'd share a room with her, but he thought better of it.

"I can put another bed in Mr. Hadigan's room, but your room is the larger of the two. However, if you insist on being alone . . . at least you're a permanent boarder, and I did agree to rent you the entire room."

"Mrs. Davenport," Buck tried to find the best way to say what he wanted to say, "before I moved in here I had a three-room ranch house to myself. I like havin' at least one room of my own. Now . . . if you're havin' trouble buyin' groceries or anything, I can maybe shell out a couple more dollars a week, or somethin'."

"No," she said. "I'm having no trouble. At least for the time being. However, if the price of groceries goes up . . ." She shrugged, stood, went to the kitchen sink and began scraping dirty dishes. He watched the way her hips moved.

It was the bartender in the Royal Flush who had a definite opinion about Spooky Hallows. Sheets was the bartender's name, a tall thin man with a handlebar moustache and black hair combed straight back.

24

"Know what I think, I think he's dead."

Buck was sipping his morning shot of whiskey, making it last. One shot was all he allowed himself, and he savored every sip. Business was slow in the Royal Flush that morning.

"Uh-huh," Buck grunted.

"Sure. Some bushwhacker found him a-digging and pumped a .40-60 in his back. You watch. Somebody'll come down from the hills a-leading old Spooky's jackasses and a-hollering that he struck 'er rich. Some a these gents around here'll recognize the jackasses, but they'll never find Spooky's remains and they'll never be able to prove he was backshot."

"You think some killer's gonna get rich off Spooky's hard labor, huh?"

"Won't be the first time. Won't be the first time a-tall."

"Uh-huh." Buck finished his whiskey and set the glass down on the hand-carved mahogany bar. He glanced at himself in the long mirror behind Sheets and then at the painting of a naked lady over the bar. God, what a pair of jugs. No woman could tote those around without being stooped-shouldered.

"Another'n?"

Smacking his lips, Buck said, "Naw." Outside, he pulled his hat down to keep the morning sun out of his eyes, stood on the sidewalk and watched the traffic go by. There was a time when he'd have had another and another and ended the night by shooting holes in all the store signs. He'd outgrown that stuff finally. Had to when a bank robber put a bullet in him. Now all he could do was sit on the porch of the boarding house and talk about the old days.

Thinking about it, Buck Innes was lonesome for Andy Hallows. He and Andy were about the only ones left around here who remembered the old days.

25

Hadigan was a miner. He didn't know cows from cowshit. Mrs. Davenport, all she could talk about was the Savior and the big tent that some folks called a church. She was always quoting the Bible and the preacher.

He was thinking about old Spooky when he saw Spooky's daughter again. She was wearing the same gray dress and a kind of vest. The little hat was pinned to the top of her blond head. She walked looked down, scowling at the splintered planks in the sidewalk, coming toward him.

"Mornin', Miss Hallows."

"Oh." She seemed startled to see him standing there. "Uh, good morning, Mr. Innes."

"Fine mornin'."

Stopping before him, she said, "Yes, it is. It's beautiful up here. The mountains are very beautiful."

She seemed to be waiting for him to say something more, but he didn't know what to say. Then she said, "I'm considering going up there to look for my father. I wonder if you would be so kind as to point me in the right direction."

"Oh, you can't do that, Miss Hallows. You'd get lost. There's an awful lot of country up there. Men that know the mountains have tried to find Spooky, er, Andy."

"I was wondering, are there any bears or tigers or anything like that up there?"

"Most of the bears are little black boogers that're more scared of people than people are of them. The painters've never hurt a man, though they're hell on burros."

"Painters?"

"Yeah, uh, panthers. Mountain lions." He wondered whether he should apologize for saying hell.

"Oh, my."

"Anyway, you don't want to go up there by yourself. You don't want to go up there at all."

"But I can't just . . . wait."

"I've been thinkin', Miss Hallows, you said some of Spooky's letters came from Florissant?"

"Yes. At least one of his envelopes was mailed at Florissant."

"He might be over there. We all done our tradin' at Florissant before Cripple Creek was born."

"Oh, really?" Her face brightened. "I should have thought of that. I'll go there. Do you know when I can catch a train there."

"There's no railroad, but John Hundley runs two or three stages up and down that road every day. You can board the stage over at the hotel and you won't have to wait long."

"I'll do that then. Thank you, Mr. Innes."

"Oh, Miss Hallows, if I was you I'd sure go over there and take a look. Ask around. But there's no stamp mill over there for separatin' gold from the worthless rock, and his cabin's here, and . . . well, anyway I'd go ask around. There's a chance you'll find him."

She was hesitant. Then her jaw squared in determination. "I have to do whatever I can. Thank you again, Mr. Innes."

After she left, hurrying toward her hotel, Buck was doubtful. Did he send her on a trip for nothing? Probably did. But . . . well, if he was looking for old Spooky that's the first place he'd look. That would be a hell of a lot smarter than going up in those hills. But she'd be back. She'd be back and disappointed. What was he going to do then?

Feeling no pain in his right hip this morning, Buck Innes walked over to the south side of town to

George Hinson's barn. Hinson had a few stables and pens and a hundred-acre pasture of good grass that he kept some of the locals' horses in. Though Buck didn't ride much anymore, he kept one horse handy in case he needed to go somewhere he couldn't go in a stage or on a train.

"Mornin', George."

"Mornin', Buck. How's your ass this mornin'?" Hinson was doing what stable owners did a lot of — shoveling manure.

"It still works and my brain still works. If you'd a got shot in the ass like I did your brains would've leaked out."

Leaning on his manure fork, the stable owner squinted at Buck, grinned and allowed, "I always thought you old cowmen were so tough in the ass you could stop bullets."

"Well, it didn't kill me. How's that bay horse of mine doin'?"

"He's gittin' too fat. You ought to git on 'im once in a while, Buck. Hell, you ain't been on 'im for so long you're gonna have to break 'im to ride all over again."

"I might have some work for him purty soon."

"How's that?"

"When's the last time you saw Spooky Hallows?"

"Old Spooky?" Hinson pushed back his bill cap and dragged a shirt sleeve across his forehead. "I dunno. Let's see. Come to think of it, it was a few weeks ago. Yeah, it's been a few weeks. Wonder what happened to 'im?"

"I ain't seen him for some time either, and his daughter's in town lookin' for him."

"His daughter? I didn't know he had a relative in the world."

"Yeah, he's got a daughter. Her mother took her

away when she was a little tyke. Any idea where he might be?"

"Naw. I heard he struck a vein way over west somewheres and he ain't tellin' nobody where. You gonna go look for 'im?"

"Aw, I don't know. If he's over west, he could be impossible to find. A man could go plumb to the Arkansas River without seein' a road or a deer trail or anything but a hell of a lot of mountains and canyons."

"He always comes down out of them hills ever' eight or ten days or so. If he ain't showed up lately, he's prob'ly dead."

"Yeah, prob'ly is."

Walking back to the boarding house, Buck's mind was troubled. Should he go look for his friend? Naw, that would be foolish. But they had been the best of friends once. He couldn't let a friend disappear without at least trying to find him. Spooky could be lying up there with a broken leg or a bullet in the back or something. But there wasn't a chance in a hundred of finding him. Besides, maybe his daughter would find him fat and happy in Florissant. He could be over there.

Sure. So could Saint Nicholas.

Chapter Four

There was a time when Buck Innes and some of the other idle citizens of Cripple Creek got a chuckle out of watching the stage arrive from Florissant. It was an eighteen-mile run with a stop at the Welty Ranch. The last stop was on top of the rim where a volcano millions of years ago had belched up the molten granite, and where another volcano a million years later had left some of Colorado's valuable minerals. Then came the drop down into the bowl of the old volcano with the six-horse team on a gallop. Brake shoes squealed and smoked, dogs, burros and people scrambled out of the way and coach passengers hung onto the seats, door posts and each other.

In front of the brick Palace Hotel, the teamster "Who-oed," and two pairs of hands grabbed the bridles on the lead horses. While the horses blew through flared nostrils, the teamster separated the six driving lines from his fingers and handed them to a helper. Then he climbed down from his high seat and hollered, "Welcome to Cripple Creek folks. Hope you enjoyed the ride."

They stepped out, faces white and knees weak. None of the onlookers laughed in their presence. The men were more than happy to help the ladies with their suitcases and trunks. But in the saloons a few minutes later, the jokes began.

"Haw-haw, didja see that gent with the big watch chain across his belly? I think he done dirtied his drawers."

"I didn't see him, but that woman that got out, the purty one, she hung on me like I was a long lost lover boy. Hell, I didn't see nothin' else."

"Barkeep, pour another'n."

Now that Hundley was running stages every few hours to keep up with the fast growing demand, it was old hat.

Buck Innes was hoping she wouldn't be on the stage, but she was. Her hands were trembling a little when he took the tin suitcase from her. There was no use asking. He could tell by her face that she hadn't found her father. In the hotel lobby, he sat in a chair beside hers and listened to her talk about the trip.

"A gentleman in Castello's store said he would recognize my father if he saw him but he hadn't seen him since early spring. Nobody at the postoffice knew anything about him. I sent a gentleman into a, uh, liquor emporium to ask. I even asked of a man on the street, a man who looked like a prospector. There's no trace of him."

"I shouldn't have sent you over there. It seemed like a good idea, but it was a dumb one."

She put a hand on his arm. "Don't blame yourself, Mr. Innes. It was the logical thing to do."

He was silent, then, "What're you gonna do now, Miss Hallows?"

"I'll have to give up, I guess. It cost me so much in stage fare to Florissant and back. I . . . I've got enough money left to go home to Denver and look for work, but that's about all." She sat slumped in

31

her chair.

"It was my dumb idea, sendin' you to Florissant, and I want to pay your fare. I ain't got but a few bucks in my pocket, but I'll get some money for you."

"I don't want to take any money from anyone. As I said, I have some funds left, but I have to spend conservatively."

"It's the least I can do for Andy's daughter. Wish I could do more."

"You could go look for him." She was studying his face, hoping for a positive sign.

"Miss Hallows," Buck matched her gaze, "if I thought there was a fair chance, I'd go. I'd go in a minute."

"Would you, Mr. Innes?"

Now he had to look away.

"Is there any chance at all?"

"Oh, I reckon a feller could hope to get lucky, but that's what it'd take, a lot of luck."

"Would you?"

Shaking his head, he said, "I'm afraid it would be a long ride for nothin'."

"I'll go with you."

"Oh no. No, you can't do that. I've only got one horse. I can borrow a pack horse, I reckon, but I've only got one bedroll, and it's no fun campin' in those hills, and a lady could get hurt, and . . ."

"But he's my father. Can't I rent a horse? And buy a bedroll? I want to do everything I can."

"No. No, you can't go with me. I work best alone."

"Then you'll go?"

"Well, I . . . I'll think about it."

"You will?" Her face brightened and she sat up straight in her chair. "Wonderful."

32

"I only said I'd think about it."

"When will you start? Tomorrow?"

"Well, I . . . I don't know. I'll have to get some groceries together and stuff. My old bed tarp ain't been used for so long it prob'ly leaks."

"Day after tomorrow?"

He knew he was being pushed and if it had been anyone but an old friend's daughter he'd have got up and walked away. Instead, all he could do was sputter. "Well, I, uh, I reckon."

"Where will you start from?"

"Don't know. Ain't thought about that yet."

"Where was the last place he was seen?"

"Well, the men that tried to follow him lost him on the other side of the graveyard."

"Wouldn't that be the place to start, then?"

"Prob'ly." He had to swallow a lump in his throat. Why was he allowing himself to be pushed into this? "I'll have to give it some thought."

"Will I see you tomorrow?"

"I reckon. I'll get some stuff together."

Her hand was on his arm and the blue eyes were locked onto his face. "My father is very fortunate to have a friend like you, Mr. Innes. And I'm very fortunate too. I'll be praying for you both."

And then he knew why.

In his narrow bed that night, in his private room at Mrs. Davenport's boarding house, he tried to map out a plan in his mind. Old Spooky had always disappeared in the timber west of the cemetery. He had to have gone in one of three different directions from there. If he'd gone far enough east he'd have got to the Arkansas Valley and the Arkansas River. South, and he could have gone clear to Canon City. North, hell, he could have gone plumb to Canada. What chance did a man have of finding him? None. None

33

at all.

Unless.

Unless old Spooky wanted to be found.

And that was the only chance Buck Innes had. If Spooky was alive and well he'd see Buck before Buck saw him. Maybe he'd recognize an old friend and holler, wave his hat or something.

If he was hurt, maybe he'd crawled out into the open country where he could be seen.

If he was dead, well, all Buck could hope to do was to find the gent leading Spooky's burros, get the drop on him, shove a gun barrel up his nose and make him tell where he left the body.

If Spooky had been murdered and Buck caught up with the killer, there would be no trial. Not even an arrest. Only quick justice.

When Mrs. Davenport heard about Buck's plan, she wanted to help. "I think you're doing the right thing, Mr. Innes, by not giving up on an old friend. I'll pack some boiled potatoes for you. Boiling potatoes must be terribly difficult over an open fire in this altitude. It takes forever to boil anything. Once they're boiled you can slice and fry them. I've got a clean lard I can put them in. And I'm going to bake today. You can take some fresh bread with you."

"Yeah, I think I'll borrow a pack horse from George Hinson. That way I can carry a bed with a mattress and plenty of chuck."

"Wanta borry my 30-30?" Hadigan asked. "It's a better gun that that old smoke pole you've got. Ever'body's braggin' about the new 30-30s."

"I'd appreciate it," Buck said. "I'll carry my .45 sixshooter too. No tellin' what I'll find up there. I'll be doing darned good if I find anything."

The first thing Buck did was catch his bay horse

and check his feet. He'd shod the horse that spring, and was relieved to see that the shoes had plenty of wear left and the hooves hadn't grown over them. Buck was at the age where shoeing horses was hard work, but he'd be damned if he'd pay someone to do it for him. When he'd shod the horse he'd had to shoe the forefeet one day, give his knees and back a rest, and shoe the hind feet the next day, but he'd got it done and kept his pride. He arranged to borrow a pack horse and pack outfit from Hinson. Next he went grocery shopping.

Ranch cooks thought it was a disgrace to open tin cans for a meal, but Buck intended to make it as easy on himself as he could, and he bought some hermetically sealed cans of tomatoes, beef, fruit, oysters and marmalade. He also bought two thick slabs of salt-cured boarbelly bacon. It kept longer than fresh meat. Back at the boarding house, he laid out his old bed tarp, saw it was ragged in places but serviceable. He laid a thin mattress on one end of it, put three blankets on the mattress and folded the other end of the tarp back over it. He folded the sides of the tarp over the middle of the bed and tied it all together with a pair of old broken bridle reins.

His spurs and stovepipe chaps were stored in a wooden box in Mrs. Davenport's shed, and he decided to leave them there. If he'd been chasing cattle he wouldn't have considered getting on a horse without spurs and chaps, but as it was he might have to do some walking. No use carrying extra weight.

At mid-afternoon Anita Hallows came puffing up the path to the boarding house, wearing the same gray dress. "Afternoon, Miss Hallows," Buck said.

"Good afternoon, Mr. Innes. You haven't changed your mind, have you?" She climbed the steps and accepted his invitation to occupy Hadigan's empty

35

chair.

"Nope, I'm ready. I'll pull out first thing in the mornin'."

"You're going to start at the cemetery, you said?"

"Yep."

"Which way will you go from there?"

"Think I'll go up to the top of Signal Mountain. You can see for fifty miles in all directions from up there."

"Is that the peak that some people call Mount Pisgah?"

"Yep. We called 'er Signal Mountain before these dandies came around and gave everything a fancy name. The Utes usta send smoke signals from up there."

"I see. Hmm. Well, I'm greatly relieved that you are going. Whether you succeed or not, I will always be very grateful."

"Don't get your hopes up, Miss Hallows."

"It's just a relief to know that someone is doing something."

She stayed only a few minutes and left, hurrying down the path toward Bennett Avenue. Buck wondered why she was in such a hurry, but he didn't give it much thought. Mrs. Davenport came out, wiping her hands on her long apron. "Was that Mr. Hallows' daughter?"

"Yep. Purty, ain't she?"

"She certainly didn't stay long. If I'd known she was out here I'd have invited her to dinner."

"She's got troubles on her mind."

"Well, if my father were missing, I would worry too. I hope you find him alive and well."

After Miss Hallows left, Buck went to the backyard and chopped four armloads of wood for the kitchen stove. He and Hadigan took turns doing that, and Buck, knowing he wouldn't be here to do his share, chopped three-days' supply. Then he went to Hinson's stables, saddled his bay horse and the sorrel pack horse and rode back to the boarding house. It felt good to be horseback again. Sure beat walking — as long as the old bullet wound behaved itself. At the boarding house he loaded his groceries and cooking utensils in the pack panniers and put his bed across the load. Then he rode back to the stables and unsaddled. He was ready now.

In his bed after supper, he wondered when he would again get to sleep in a bed with springs, and it occurred to him that maybe he never would. Men had gone into those mountains and had never come back. Spooky Hallows had disappeared up there and he knew the mountains as well as anybody. Aw, well hell, Buck, he said to himself, if all you're gonna do the rest of your life is set out there on the porch, or inside by the stove, you ain't got much of a life anyhow.

Mrs. Davenport was up before daylight fixing his breakfast. He stuffed himself with hotcakes, sausage and scalding coffee. It would be his last woman-cooked meal for who knows how long. When he left, carrying the borrowed 30-30 rifle and his Colt .45 Peacemaker, she said:

"I'll pray for you, Mr. Innes."

Why not, he said to himself as he walked down the path toward Bennet Avenue, it prob'ly won't do no good but it sure can't do no harm either.

Chapter Five

It had been many months since he'd been up this early and the air was downright cold. He buttoned his blanket-lined denim jacket and turned the collar up. Fingers numb with cold, he saddled the horses and tied his bed on top of the crossbuck saddle with a lash cinch. George Hinson was there, but answered with only a grunt when Buck asked him why he was up so early. The sun was just showing itself over the volcanic rim behind him when he rode out of town and past the cemetery. The tallest tombstones were casting long shadows and were ghostly in the early light. He heard a steam whistle somewhere and knew it was time for some of the miners to go to work.

Hell, he said to himself, I could be worse off. I could be goin' down one of those mine shafts and spendin' the day muckin' in the mud and rocks. Bein' horseback is a hell of a lot better than that. In fact, as he rode, he felt good. The bullet wound wasn't bothering him, his bay horse was frisky and stepping right along, the pack horse was leading easy, the air was clean and smelled good, and the sky was cloudless.

A Steller's jaybird, looking like a bandit wearing a black hood—topknot and all—lit on a pine limb ahead of him and gave him a good scolding. A furry, striped little chipmunk hurried out of his way. A black squirrel with long ears ran half-way up a ponderosa, stopped and watched him. Buck Innes felt like humming, even singing. In fact, he did, half under his breath: "Oh, the Camp Town race track five miles long. Doo-dah, doo-dah. Oh, the Camp Town . . ."

Suddenly, he reined up, squinting. A man sat on a horse at the edge of the pine and spruce, watching him. A strange looking little man in baggy overalls and a big black hat. He had leather saddlebags hanging behind the cantle of his saddle and a rolled-up sleeping bag on top of the saddlebags.

"Who in the humped up hell . . . ?" And Buck groaned. "Oh no. It can't be. Aw, for cryin' in the road."

He rode on and when he was within talking distance he groaned again and said, "Miss Hallows, what the heck are you doin' here?"

The new black hat covered her blond hair, but her smooth, hairless, round face made her easy to recognize. The overalls covered her figure, but the hands poking out of the sleeves of an old plaid mackinaw were small, feminine. The mackinaw was the one that had been hanging in Spooky's cabin. She smiled.

"I told you I want to go along."

"Where'd you get the horse and outfit?"

"From Mr. Hinson."

"How come he didn't tell me about that?"

"I got him to promise not to."

"Why, that son-of-a-buck. That's why he wouldn't talk to me this mornin'."

39

The round smooth face turned serious. "I really do want to go along, Mr. Innes. I can't just sit and wait and worry. I won't be any trouble, I promise."

"There ain't no way you can't be no trouble."

"I can chop wood and cook and I brought a sleeping bag and some food and I promise I won't get in your way."

"Aw-w-w."

"Please, Mr. Innes."

He felt like turning around and going right back. Looking for Spooky Hallows by himself would be next to impossible. Dragging this girl with him would be . . . wait a minute. "Hmm," he mused aloud.

"Please." The pale blue eyes were pleading too.

"Hmm. Take off that hat."

"What? Take off my hat? Why?"

"You gonna argue with me?"

"No, uh, all right, if you say so." When she lifted the hat, her blond hair shone in the morning sun. Her hair was cut short, but it was longer than a man's hair, obviously a woman's.

Buck studied the effect and a small smile turned up one corner of his mouth. "All right, but keep that hat off. Except when it rains and hails."

"Would you mind telling my why?"

" 'Cause if old Spooky sees us, he might recognize you. He'll at least know you're a female."

"Oh, I see. Of course. Why didn't I think of that?"

Reining his horse around her he went on, leading the pack horse. She fell in behind. It was uphill from there, through the pine, spruce and aspen, over a narrow, rocky trail. Buck's happy mood was gone, and he was silent. She kept quiet too. The trail dipped into a narrow, shallow draw, then rose steeper than before. Soon they were out in the sun again, riding along the side of a steep rocky hill. There were no tracks on the trail. No sign of anything human. At one point, the hill above them was covered with broken lava rock, each rock about the size of a man's head. It was the result of a rock slide hundreds of years earlier.

Buck glanced up at it, then kept his head down, thinking about how ironic it would be if those rocks decided to break loose and slide again. Some day the rain and snowmelt would loosen the soil enough that they would.

Steadily climbing, they rode through the brushy cinquefoil with its tiny yellow flowers, through more aspen with shimmering leaves, and thick stands of pine and spruce. Halfway up to the peak, they could look down behind them and see the open country beyond the cemetery. Buck reined up to let the horses blow. The girl stopped behind the pack horse. Looking down, Buck suddenly half-turned in his saddle, eyes narrowed.

Her eyes followed his gaze. "What? What is it, Mr. Innes?"

He didn't answer for a moment, then sat straight again. "Aw nothin'."

"Did you see someone?"

"Naw." But after he kicked his mount with spurless bootheels and went on, climbing, he glanced back now and then.

It wasn't far to the top of Mount Pisgah, but it was steep, and Buck stopped every hundred yards or so to let the horses get their wind. Every time he stopped he studied the scenery behind them. They were following an Indian trail, and Buck marveled at how the Indians had always found the best routes to anywhere. In the grazing lands, cattle were good trailmakers, but cattle had never climbed up here. This trail was made by the deer, elk and Indians.

Finally, they were at the top, at the edge of an acre-sized volcanic bowl. A thousand years earlier molten rock had spewed out of a fissure in the earth and piled up to form the peak with a hollow top. Now the bowl was cool and shallow enough that a man could walk down into it. Near the edge, where there was a small level spot, Buck dismounted, unloaded the pack horse and loosened all the saddle cinches. Anita Hallows almost fell when her feet touched the ground, and she groaned as she regained her balance and some strength in her legs. The old wound in Buck's right hip was beginning to ache, and he felt like groaning too, but he only clenched his teeth. The sun was halfway up to its zenith. They had a lot more riding to do that day.

"My gosh," the girl exclaimed after walking to the top. "You can see everywhere. Just look at that."

From where they stood they could see Pikes Peak to the east by northeast, the Sangre de Christos to the south and the Continental Divide far to the west. It was a spectacular view. But what interested Buck was the canyons away downhill to the north, with cliffs that went almost straight up, and the timbered canyon to the south. To the west—the near west—the country was too open, bare of timber, no place for a hidden gold mine. He could see what remained of his family's old homestead ranch, the rock foundation and chimney. Fire had left the cabin, barn and sheds a smoke-blackened mess after he'd sold and moved to town.

Every time he rode past the place, or saw it from a high hill, he felt a lump in his throat. His dad was the first to homestead there and a year later was joined by a brother. The next year another brother came along. And when Buck was old enough he too claimed a quarter section. Now everyone was dead. They had died one at a time from a wreck with a horse, a brief gunfight with Indians, and an overturned wagon. It was pneumonia that took his mother. She was buried with the others down there near the charred remains.

A millionaire from Denver had once planned to build a hunting lodge there, but gave up after fire wiped it all out. Now there were no cattle on the old homesteads. Good grass was going to waste. The familiar lump rose in Buck's throat again. If he were a little younger he'd try to buy back the place and return to ranching.

If — the biggest word in the English language.

"Where are we going from here, Mr. Innes?"

Her question jerked his mind back to Spooky Hallows. Let's see. A hidden mine had to be in one of those canyons. Either north or south. That took in a hell of a lot of country. If he went far enough east to get across the bare hills he'd come to more canyons, a lot of timber and then the Arkansas Valley and the Arkansas River. No matter which way he went, if he went far enough, he'd run into nothing but canyons, gulches, tall trees and rocky hill after rocky hill.

"Danged if I know," he answered, finally. "Your eyes are younger than mine, do you see anything that looks man-made? I mean anything north or south or west?"

"No, I don't see anything." She walked in her slouchy overalls around the bowl from one side to another. "I don't see any smoke from a campfire or anything. Do you think my father came up here?" Her blond hair gleamed in the sun.

"Naw. There's nothin' up here. I came up here to look around, is all. To try to get an idea of where he

43

went."

"You don't see any clues at all, huh? Can you make an educated guess?"

At that he had to grin. "Educated, I ain't. And my guesses are no better than anybody else's."

"But you said you know these mountains better than anyone."

"Huh," Buck snorted. "I didn't say that. Hadigan said that."

"Then what are we doing?" Her voice carried a hint of irritation. And that didn't help Buck's mood.

"I'm doin' what you wanted me to do. Right now I'm tryin' to think."

"All right. I'm sorry."

He didn't look her way. Instead he walked to the western edge of the hollow and tried to put his mind to work. Let's see. If he was going north or south, he would have been in open country for a few miles. If he wanted to disappear he'd keep heading west by southwest and stay in the timber. Yeah, he was headed west every time he was seen leavin' town, so he must be southwest of here. Or . . .

He would have known he was bein' followed, and he might have gone into the timber just to lose whoever was following him. So which way did he go from there? He always left town at night. Did he cross open country in the dark? He wouldn't have tried to cross those canyons at night.

Goddamnit. Might as well spit in the wind and see which way it blows.

The girl was quiet, watching him. There was no grass on top of the peak, and the horses had nothing to do but stand with their heads down, stomp their feet and switch their tails at the flies.

All right. Old Spooky always left in the night. He didn't want anybody to see which way he went. What time of night? Think. Did somebody say once he followed Spooky out of town to the graveyard about an hour after dark? If that was so, maybe the old sourdough planned on gettin' across some open country before daylight. Let's see. Miss Hallows said somebody in Florissant had seen him last spring. That's north. To get there he'd have to cross some open hills, but once he did that he could duck into the tall timber again and get into some rough country. And if he took off to the northwest, he'd be hidden from anybody but an eagle.

Without speaking, Buck went back to the horses, tightened the cinches and reloaded the pack horse.

"Are we leaving, Mr. Innes? Which way are we going?"

"Northwest." Then he pulled the 30-30 out of the saddle boot and walked back to the southeast side. Kneeling on one knee, he tugged his hat brim down to shade his eyes and watched, squinting.

"What's happening? What are you doing?"

He didn't answer. Instead he put the gun to his shoulder and fired without taking aim. The explosion split the quiet, and the sound rolled out over the tall trees and hills.

"Mr. Innes, what did you do that for?" She was ready to clap her hands over her ears if he fired again.

Instead, he replaced the rifle in its boot on the left side of the bay horse and mounted before he answered, "That's to let those jaspers down there know we know they're there."

Chapter Six

He rode downhill leading the pack horse, letting his saddle horse pick its way over the rocks. Only once did he glance back to see if the girl was following him. She was far behind, just getting on her horse. He didn't stop for her. In places they had to traverse the peak, almost turning back on themselves. By noon they were out of the timber where the grass was high and could be pushed down by horses' hooves, leaving an easy trail to follow. The land was still steep here, though, and covered in places with volcanic rocks as big as a saddle. The bay horse had been raised in that country, and knew to pick its way carefully. Then they were off the peak and down on some of the Innes family's old grazing land. The girl had been quiet until then, but now she spoke:

"Are we going to stop for lunch, Mr. Innes?"

"Nope. Not here." He glanced back at her again. She was staying behind the pack horse, hanging onto the saddle horn, obviously tiring. Maybe, he thought, he ought to stop and let her rest. But no, by God, he'd warned her about coming along. In fact, he'd told her not to. She'd get tired and her ass would get sore, but she was young. She'd live.

And thinking of sore asses, goddamnit, his right hip was aching steadily now.

Off to their left about a mile, the country tilted again and was covered with tall pine and spruce. He reined in that direction. No one had been over this land in recent weeks, he was sure of that. Looking back, he could see where the horses' hooves had tromped down the tall grass, and he knew from experience the grass would stay down until the next hard rain. In another eight weeks deep snow would flatten it and only next spring's sunshine would bring it to life again. Spooky hadn't come this way. To their right a couple of miles was the stage road to Florissant. If Spooky had traveled anywhere near the road he would have been seen. No, if he came north at all, he came northwest. Buck didn't look back again until they were in the timber at least three miles from the stage road. Then he searched for a place to rest the horses.

Finally, he reined up and turned his horse around. "There's a creek west of here about a mile. We'll stop there for a while. How you doin'?"

Her face was pinched, but she managed a weak smile. "I'm staying with you."

"Good," he said, and went on.

When they came to a narrow draw that ran southwest through the woods, he stopped again. A creek, not much more than a trickle, ran down the length of the draw. He dismounted, and walked with a limp a few steps until the ache in his hip subsided. It was good to walk. The girl dismounted with a loud groan, and again almost fell. She too had to walk a few steps before she quit staggering.

"I brought some canned peaches, Mr. Innes. Won't that make a good lunch?"

"Yeah, it'll do." He unloaded the pack horse again and loosened the cinches. Then he led the three horses down to the creek. The horses managed to suck enough moisture between their wide lips to quench their thirst. Buck went upstream, lay on his belly and drank the same way, sucking the water up between his lips. Anita Hallows knelt beside him and dipped a tin cup into the water.

What with two cups of coffee that morning and now a drink of water, Buck's bladder was about to pop. Embarrassed, he told the girl, "You're gonna have to excuse me a minute," and he walked away, headed for the other side of a big ponderosa. "It's quite all right," she said. And when Buck came back, after carefully buttoning his pants, he saw that she too had gone somewhere to empty her bladder.

"This damn campin' with a woman has got problems I don't need," he muttered to himself. "A man can't even take a pee when he wants to."

When she returned, they sat on the ground and ate two cans of peaches, which made her saddle bags lighter and less bulky. Buck stood, felt a sharp pain flare up then die down in his right hip, and walked back the way they had come. He walked about four hundred yards, stopped, looked and listened. He neither saw nor heard anyone. Back at the horses, he tightened the cinches, reloaded the pack horse and mounted.

"Which way are we going from here, Mr. Innes?"

"Northwest. Mostly west," he said.

As they rode on, across the draw, he looked back and saw the two empty tin cans on the ground. He'd thought about hiding them, but figured it was useless. It couldn't be helped, they were leaving a trail a blind man could follow.

They came to their first deep canyon at mid-afternoon. Buck rode into it, but not far. The bottom was so rocky and steep a horse couldn't travel on it. He turned around and rode back out. The girl followed him. At the mouth of the canyon he dismounted, walked and led the horses a few steps then leaned against the saddle horn to ease the pain in his hip.

"What now, Mr. Innes?"

"A horse can't go in there, but maybe a burro could. I didn't see no sign of anything. I think I'll walk in there a ways and see what there is to see. You wait here. Can you hang onto the horses?"

"I . . . I'll try." She dismounted sorely. He handed her the reins to his bay horse.

"Well, hang onto at least one of 'em." Then, shifting the gun belt to get the .45 in a more comfortable position on his hip, he started walking. He'd been in the canyon before, but years ago. He remembered that it was dry except after a hard rain or in the early spring when the snow melted. This was not the kind of place he expected to find gold. But he'd seen prospector's holes in the ground in lots of places where there was no water and nothing interesting that he could see. Climbing over and around waist-high boulders, he went about four hundred yards into the canyon and saw no sign of anyone else having been there.

He had to admit to himself that he was tiring too when he made his way back to the girl and the horses. His saddle horse and the pack horse were free, but were cropping the grass nearby, and he had no trouble catching them.

"Nobody's been in there for a long time," he said. "Let's get horseback again."

They rode along the side of a hill that was bare of timber, then rode into the timber again in a narrow valley. Here, there was another creek, one of many that started at the Continental Divide and traveled all the way to the Arkansas. Buck stopped, studied the terrain around them, then rode up the creek. Someone had been there. Someone had done some panning.

"See that?" he said to the girl.

"What is it?"

"See them shallow holes dug in the bottom of the creek? Some prospector has been scoopin' up sand and gravel and hopin' to find some color here."

"Could it have been my father?"

"Don't think so. 'Cuz whoever it was didn't find anything. And it wasn't too long ago. Runnin' water would've filled up those holes." Buck shifted in the saddle to put most of his weight on his left hip. "Spooky, er, Andy, found his vein long before this creek was panned."

"Is that an old campfire over there?" Anita Hallows pointed to some black ashes on the bank of the creek.

"Yep. And the gent didn't have no burros. He had to carry everything on his back."

"My father had burros, you said?"

"Yep."

"Where are we going to spend the night?"

"Let's go downstream a ways." He turned his horses around and went back the way they'd come. They followed the creek until it went into another narrow canyon. Buck knew where the creek came out of the canyon, on the other side of a timbered ridge, and he headed his horses for the top of that ridge. Again, they had to traverse the hill to get to the top, winding their way around granite boulders as big as

50

a wagon. At the top, Buck stopped long enough to study the terrain below them. He saw where the creek came out of the canyon up ahead. Nobody was behind them. The sun was about to set on the horizon to the west. "Down there by the creek is a good place to camp," he allowed. "Let's get down there."

Winding their way down the hill, sometimes in the woods and sometimes in the open, the girl groaned again and hung onto the saddle horn. Buck knew without looking back what was bothering her. A horse's front hooves hit the ground harder going downhill and that jolted the rider more. Finally, Buck did look back. "Push on the saddle horn, Miss Hallows. Push. Make it easy on yourself." He was putting most of his weight on the stirrups and pushing on his own saddle horn.

At the bottom, they rode into a stand of ponderosas and picked up the creek again. There too, they found signs of gold panning and of someone camping. There was only one set of boot prints, and no burro tracks.

"Whoever that jasper is, he ain't havin' no luck," Buck mused. "And judgin' from these tracks, his feet're about to come out of his boots. Looks like he's pannin' every place the creek comes out of a canyon."

Anita Hallows wasn't talking. When she got off her horse she collapsed on the ground and didn't move, only groaned.

Limping slightly from the ache in his hip, Buck unloaded the pack horse and unsaddled the three animals. He hobbled their front feet and also sidelined his bay horse. "Got to make sure we've got at least one horse in the mornin'," he said, as much to himself as to anyone else. The mountain grass was plentiful and the horses got busy grazing, moving with short awkward hop-steps. "You just rest easy, Miss Hallows. I'll fix us somethin' to eat."

She was lying flat on her back with her big hat for a pillow. "I don't think I can move," she groaned.

"Ridin' up and down the hills takes muscles it don't take ridin' on the prairie. I've known prairie cowboys that got so stove up ridin' these hills that they walked funny for a couple of days."

Gathering firewood was easy in the pine country. The lower limbs were always dead and easy to break off. Soon he had a fire going and a skillet sitting over two rocks. He took a slab of bacon out of his pack panniers and used his belt knife to cut off two thick slices. While the bacon sizzled he filled his coffee pot in the creek.

"That jasper's hopin' to find some color where the water comes out of the canyons," Buck said, conversationally, trying to ignore the ache in his hip. "If he does, he'll prob'ly figure it's comin' from a vein up in the canyon somewheres and he'll break his back tryin' to find that vein."

Without moving her head, she grunted and said, "What's a vein?"

"Oh, it's just a crack in the rock that got filled up with gold a million years ago when the world was so hot it melted the soft stuff. Gold is soft. Even I know that, and I don't know nothin' about prospectin'."

"How do you know the world was once so hot?"

"Oh, there was a mining engineer stayed at Mrs. Davenport's boardin' house once and he talked about that stuff."

With another long groan, the girl sat up, sat cross-legged and rested her elbows on her knees. "I'm too tired to eat but I'm starved."

"We'll have some chuck here in a little bit. What

kind of a bed have you got?"

"It's a long sack made out of heavy quilts. You have to unbutton it to get in it, then you button it up again."

Shaking his head, Buck allowed. "I've seen some of these old sourdoughs head for the hills with nothin' more'n a couple of blankets for a bed. Not me. Good thing the Almighty made pack horses. It takes a good stout horse to carry my bed."

Their meal consisted of bacon, a can of peas, bread with plum preserves and boiled coffee. While there was still some daylight left, Buck washed the dishes in the creek. The girl didn't offer to help. After dark, when the only light was the firelight, Buck opened his bed away from the fire, under a ponderosa. He considered offering to help the girl with her bed, but, hell, if she couldn't do that much for herself she'd better go back where she came from. His hip was throbbing a little, but not enough to keep him awake, and he dozed off within a half-hour.

When he woke up it was daylight and he was looking up the bore of a gun.

Chapter Seven

Buck Innes sat up with a snort. His thick gray hair was sticking out in all directions. His eyes were wild. "Who the holy hell are you?"

"The question is," the man said, "who the hell are you?" He was short and wide, with a week's growth of brown whiskers and dark hollows under his eyes. He wore a floppy black hat and baggy wool pants held up with red suspenders. The gun in his hand looked to be a Civil War model six-shooter. The hammer was back and the man's finger was on the trigger. "And who's that other gent over there?"

"That there is a woman, and we ain't done nobody no harm and we ain't got nothin' worth stealin'. If it's horses you're after, every mother's son in southern Colorado knows those horses. If you're seen with 'em you'll be hung."

"A woman, you say? What're you doin' here?"

Buck wanted to stand up, but the gun was aimed right at his face and it didn't waver. "We're lookin' for somebody, that's what." His own gun was in its holster hanging from the limb of a tree over his head. The 30-30 was by the camp ashes with the pack panniers.

"You the law?"

"Nope. We ain't got nothin' to do with the law."

"What's a woman doin' here?"

"We're lookin' for her pappy."

"Her pappy?" The callused hand holding the gun relaxed a little. "What're you lookin' for her pappy for?"

This was getting exasperating. "Because she wants to see him, that's what for."

"Is he lost?"

"Naw, he ain't lost."

"Are you lost?"

"Hell no."

"Well." The man seemed to ponder that a moment. "Well, you're on my claim and that makes you a trespasser. I got a right to protect my claim."

"I didn't see no markers, and we ain't lookin' for gold anyhow."

Finally, the gun hand dropped and the gun was pointed at the ground. "I don't mean nobody no harm. I'm just protectin' my claim."

Buck pushed the bed tarp and blankets off and swung his feet out onto the ground. He reached under the foot of the tarp for his boots and pulled them on. Standing, he unbuttoned his pants, tucked his shirt tail in, then rebuttoned them. With satisfaction he noticed that the three horses were grazing near the creek where the grass was highest. "Hell of a way to wake up, a gun in my face." He nodded toward the still-sleeping girl, covered to the top of her head with a heavy quilt. "Good thing you didn't point a gun at her, you'd have scared the hell out of her."

"I didn't mean nobody no harm. I'm just protectin' my claim. You, uh, you got any spare grub?"

"Yeah. If you'll put that cannon away I'll fix somethin' to eat." He reached for the gunbelt hanging from a tree, saw the man stiffen, and decided to leave the gun where it was. "When did you run out of chuck?"

"Yestiday mornin'. I'm gonna hoof it back to town, but I run out of money too. I thought I could kill somethin' to eat, but I ain't seen nothin' bigger'n a gopher."

"They don't taste too good," Buck said, walking with a slight limp to the pack panniers. "I'll get a fire goin' and wake her up." He broke off some more dead limbs and soon had a fire crackling. Then he went over to the sleeping form. She was on her side with her knees drawn up, her face buried. Buck wondered how she kept from suffocating.

"Hey, Miss Hallows," Buck said. She didn't move. Maybe she did suffocate. "Hey, you alive?" Still no movement. Squatting beside her, he shook her shoulder. "Hey, it's daylight. Time to get up."

"Huh?" She turned over onto her back, squinted at him, closed her eyes, then opened them wider. "What? What's happened?"

"Nothin's happened. It's time to get up, that's all. And, oh yeah, we've got company."

"What?" She sat up, struggled to get her arms out of the sack, then started unhooking the big brass buttons. "What company?"

"A prospector. He's harmless."

"Oh. Where'd he come from?"

"I didn't ask him." Buck stood and looked down at her.

She was fully dressed except for her shoes. She got her feet out of the sack, pulled the shoes on and laced them. Her blond hair was wild, and she tried to comb it down with slender white fingers. The baggy shapeless clothes made her look more like a boy than a young woman.

"Breakfast'll be ready in a couple of minutes," Buck said, walking away.

He made coffee, fried more bacon and sliced some bread. With no spare plate, he offered his to the prospector. He had to pour the bacon grease out of the skillet and use it for a plate. They had no extra coffee cup either, and Buck and the girl shared one. She sat cross-legged on the cool ground and ate without speaking.

"Where'd you come from this mornin'?" Buck asked.

Nodding toward the canyon, the man spoke around a mouthful of bread. "Up yonder. Found some good color, but I run out of grub."

"I didn't see no donkey tracks. You carryin' everything on your own back?"

"Yeah. A good jackass costs too much. I run out of money down there in Cripple Creek."

"A lot of men run out of money in Cripple Creek. If the, er, if the ladies don't get it the card sharps will. So you thought you'd find gold and get rich."

"Like I said, I found some good color. I'm gonna set up some markers and file a claim."

"When did you leave Cripple Creek?"

Chewing fast and swallowing, the man said, "Six-eight days ago. Been all over up here."

"See anybody?"

"No. Did you say you're lookin' for somebody?"

"Yeah, a prospector like you. Last time anybody saw him he was leadin' two jackasses. You ain't seen nobody, huh?"

"Not nobody."

"Where all have you been?"

"Plumb over to that big valley northwest of here."

"How far north did you go?"

"Oh, a dozen miles or more, but mostly west. I didn't see no sign of nobody."

"What're you gonna do now?"

"I'm outa grub and ever'thing. Reckon I'll go back and see can I get a job muckin' in the mines. Soon's I can make a stake I'll come back here. Say, you wouldn't wanta buy a gun, would you? I can sure use a few bucks, and it's a good gun."

"I've got all the iron I wanta carry. Need some eatin' money, huh?"

"Yeah, they don't pay 'till payday."

"I don't carry much money with me. Tell you what, though, I'll give you a few dollars and you can pay me back when you get rich." Buck unbuttoned a shirt pocket and took out a small roll of bills. He peeled off a five. "Here. Add this to a couple weeks wages, and maybe you can do some more gold huntin'."

A callused hand reached for the money and quickly stuffed it into a pants pocket. "I sure do thank you, mister. My name's Harvey. William Harvey. I'll surely pay you back as soon as I can. And I'm sorry I pointed a gun at you. Say, could you maybe spare a couple of airtights? I can't go back 'till I put up some markers."

"Yeah, I can spare a couple tins of beef and some bread that's gonna turn green on us anyway. That's all we can spare though. We don't know when we're gonna get back."

"I sure do thank you." William Harvey stood. "Ma'am, I hope I wasn't too much bother. I'll wash the dishes. And I surely hope you find your pappy."

Still not speaking, she only nodded.

"Well," Buck stood too, "if you happen to see a man about my age, a man named Hallows, tell him his daughter is lookin' for him."

"Hallows? Spooky Hallows? I've heared of him. I heered he struck a rich 'un. I heered he's keepin' it a secret."

At that, Buck had to grin. "He sure is. That's why we're havin' to look for him."

"I been all over northwest of here and I seen where somebody'd done some diggin' prob'ly two-three months ago, but I didn't see nobody."

"Was there any burro sign around them diggin's?"

"Yup. I b'lieve there was one jackass."

"Are you sure the sign was at least two months old?"

"I been trompin' around the gold country for years and I'm always lookin' for sign. I know."

"Did you go south at all?"

"Nope. West and north."

The sun was shining through the trees, casting long shadows, when Buck and Anita Hallows were horseback again. She was wrapped up in her father's old mackinaw, the one they'd found hanging on a wall in his cabin, and still she shivered in the early morning chill. When they rode out of the woods into the sun, she had to stop and take the mackinaw off. Buck tied it to the fork of her saddle. Looking back, he saw William Harvey gathering rocks to build claim markers.

"No use goin' north and no use goin' straight west," Buck allowed. "Let's cut southwest. That's prob'ly our best bet."

They rode up a high treeless ridge to the top and down off the crest of the ridge. Buck reined up again. Dismounting, he handed his reins to the girl and walked back to the top, keeping low. There, he lay on his stomach and studied their backtrail a full five minutes. Then he crawled backwards until he was off the skyline, and went back to the horses. "Maybe I should've bought that feller's gun," he said. "Ever shoot a gun, Miss Hallows?"

"Me? Shoot a gun? Why, no."

Shaking his head sadly, Buck mounted and rode on, leading the pack horse. He began singing, mostly under his breath, "Oh, the Camp Town . . . doo dah."

By noon they were west and a little south of Cripple Creek, about halfway between the Shelf Road that ran from Cripple Creek to Canon City and the Arkansas River. They had been riding over rocky, boulder-strewn ridges and across narrow valleys covered with brushy cinquefoil and willow bushes. There were no trails here. Buck had to stop now and then and study the terrain to figure out which way to go. Two buck deer, antlers still a little fuzzy but turning hard, bounced like huge rubber balls across an open park. They disappeared in the woods ahead of them. At the edge of the woods Buck and Miss Hallows saw a man-dug hole in the ground.

Stopping beside it, Buck mused. "Some jasper went to a lot of work for nothin'." The hole was about ten feet deep, and dirt and rocks had been piled beside it. A ladder made of small tree trunks lay on the ground. "Yup. Dug that hole with a pick and shovel and packed the dirt up that ladder, and didn't gain a damned thing by it."

"That's a lot of hard work for nothing, huh, Mr. Innes."

"Yup. That's what your daddy done. He was lucky enough to hit somethin', but you can bet he dug a lot of worthless holes like this one too."

"Could he have dug this one?"

"Could of. This one was dug over a year ago. Rain water has carried a lot of pine needles and dirt down it. Whoever done it camped here a few weeks and he had burros."

"Does that mean we're going in the right direction?"

"It could. As I recollect, there's another creek ahead a ways. We'll stop there for a while."

Riding on, Buck tried to ignore the pain in his right hip. He hummed quietly, "Doo dah—doo dah."

Another tributary stream provided the water that the man, woman and three horses needed. Two hermetically sealed cans of fruit and two large hunks of bread provided a cold meal. While the girl lay sprawled on the grass, Buck walked up the stream a ways to see what he could see and to work the soreness out of his legs and hip. He saw nothing interesting.

After a short rest, they were riding again, hugging the stream. Buck had followed this stream before, years ago, and he knew it wound between a series of low hills, through several acres of thick willows and into a deep canyon. The canyon was another ten or twelve hours ride, and he didn't expect to reach it before dark.

"Mr. Innes, how much farther are we going today?"

"Not much farther. We'll camp on this creek somewhere. There's good grass and water. If we don't cut any sign of anybody we'll go on tomorrow to Shotgun Canyon."

They passed two more prospectors' holes, both dug at least a year earlier, and then they were in the willows. Buck pulled his hat down low, ducked his head and pushed his way through. He'd chased cattle out of these bushes and he knew how difficult it could be. A cow could put her head down and plow through them on a run while a man on a horse had to hang onto the saddle to keep from being dragged off. Buck wished now he'd brought his leather chaps.

A loud grunt behind him reminded him of Miss Hallows. Looking back, he saw her on the ground behind her horse. Dismounting, pushing his way through the brush, he went to her. "Are you hurt?"

"Of course I'm hurt. Do we have to go through these awful bushes?" Her hat was hanging from a string around her throat and her blond hair was in her face.

"Did you break anything."

"Of course I did. Aren't you going to help me up?"

"No. See if you can get up by yourself. If you can you ain't hurt. If you can't then I'll have to . . . I don't know. Somethin'."

Though her face was red with exasperation and she had a scratch on her left cheek, she got to her feet. Buck looked her over, saw no serious damage. "Can you get back on your horse?"

"I don't know. How much more of these bushes do we have to go through?"

"Try to get on your horse."

Her bad humor didn't help Buck's disposition, and when he saw the awkward way she got on a horse he just had to say something. "You're just lookin' to get hurt, Miss Hallows." Her reins were tied together to keep her from dropping them, and she let them hang on the horse's neck while she took a stirrup in both hands and put her foot in it. "If that horse decided to walk away when you got your foot in the stirrup and a hold of nothin' else, you'd get hurt and I'd have to carry you back to town. Hang onto them reins, will you?"

"Well, you might hold the horse for me."

"Danged if I will." He got on his own horse, picked up the pack horse's lead rope and rode on without looking back. Pushing, ducking, they eventually broke out of the willows and found themselves on the side of a hill with the creek below them. Buck stopped, twisted in his saddle and studied the willows behind and below them. Nothing moved. He looked at the girl. She was hanging onto the saddle horn and seemed to be unhurt. Riding on, they climbed to the crest of the hill where Buck stopped again. While the horses sucked in air through flared nostrils, he again studied the country behind them, then looked in all directions, squinting, his gray eyes taking in everything. Nothing human had been this way for some time.

"Are you mad at me, Mr. Innes?"

After thinking about it a moment, he answered with a drawl, "Naw. Reckon not. We was just raised different, that's all." He touched spurless boot heels to his horse's sides and went on, dipping now toward the stream at the bottom of the hill.

Yeah, when he thought about it he remembered being something like her once. Back when he was fourteen. It was in the spring when all the cattlemen in the territory were gathering and branding the spring calf crop. They all worked together, camping with a chuck wagon, to make certain no one burned his brand on someone else's calf. Buck wanted to go. His dad told him to stay home. Maybe he could go next year. Buck went anyway.

Just like Miss Hallows, he got on his horse with a few blankets tied behind the cattle and met his dad far enough from home that he couldn't get back before dark. At first the senior Innes threatened to whip him, then changed his mind and let him go.

But boy, did young Buck Innes earn his keep.

He rode up and down mountains until his butt was raw, gathering cattle out of the rocks, timber and brush. Often riding at a dead run trying to head off cattle before they got into the brush, hoping his mount didn't stumble on the rocks and fall. And after an area was combed for cattle, the branding—the hard work—started. Young Buck wrestled calves until he was covered with bruises and raw skinned places and was so tired he couldn't even eat his supper. Day after day for nearly a month, it went like that. It rained and it hailed. Lightning cracked and thunder boomed. He wore wet clothes and slept in a wet bed. During the day he was constantly being bitten by flies and at night he had to sleep with his head covered up to keep the mosquitos from eating him alive. Between storms, he broiled in the sun and licked chapped, sore lips. When it was finally over, he helped his dad drive their cattle back toward their homestead. That took three more days.

Yeah, like Miss Hallows he got himself into something he wished he hadn't. But on the other hand he wasn't like her. He did his share of the work no matter how he felt, and he didn't complain.

At the bottom of the hill now, they followed the stream until it entered thick timber, a dark and mysterious woods. Buck dismounted sorely, rubbed his right hind cheek a moment, then unloaded the pack horse and unsaddled. The girl had been quiet. Now she spoke.

"Mr. Innes, I'm sorry. I wish I knew how to do

these things. If you'll tell me how, I'll do whatever I can. I don't want to be any bother."

"Aw," he grumbled, "it's all right. We was just fetched up different, that's all."

"You asked me if I could shoot a gun, why did you ask that?"

He didn't know whether to tell her. Looking down, he mulled it over. Then he said, "Miss Hallows, you might as well know. Somebody's trailin' us. I don't know who they are, but I got a suspicion what they want. They ain't friends."

Chapter Eight

A brief rain fell just before sundown. Lightning flashed to the west. Buck saw it coming and managed to get his bed under a tree and Miss Hallows' sleeping bag inside one of the canvas panniers before the first fat drops fell. The small fire Buck had built was quickly doused. The rain lasted only a few minutes and the clouds moved on. Walking into the dark woods, Buck broke off enough low tree limbs to get another fire going. He boiled coffee and fried bacon. They ate all but the last hunk of their bread.

"Thank goodness you had the foresight to keep our beds dry," Miss Hallows said.

"You sleep in a wet bed once, and you think of things like that."

In the morning, the sky was clear. By sunup they were riding again. Buck's old bullet wound ached steadily, and he decided that when they got to Shotgun Canyon they'd stop for the night no matter how early it was. At mid-afternoon, after riding down a steep hill and through more willows, they came to it.

Shotgun Canyon was so-named because it was as straight as a gun barrel with overhanging cliffs in places and boulders as big as houses seeming to grow out of the hills elsewhere. After the horses were hobbled and firewood was gathered, Buck walked into the canyon far enough that he had to look straight up to see the sky. In here the sun shone for maybe two hours a day in the summer and not at all in the winter. The stream ran straight and could be followed by a man on a horse. Except after a thunderstorm. Then it was so deep and swift it rolled boulders around in its bottom. Cattle had been easy to drive through here in dry weather because there was no place for them to go but straight ahead. There were no cattle in this territory now. Everyone was trying to get rich in the mines. Good grazing land was going to waste.

A quarter mile into the canyon, Buck saw tracks. Man tracks. Burro tracks. They were in a wide spot where grass grew along the creek, one of the few wide spots in the bottom of Shotgun Canyon. There were also the remains of a campfire and an empty sardine can. The can was shiny. The tracks and burro droppings were not fresh but not old either. Someone had spent the night here and it was since the last hard rain. A flash flood would have washed away any sign of a camp. Yet—Buck walked around and studied the creek—whoever it was did no panning. He wasn't looking for color. Besides, a prospector would pan the creek where it came out of a canyon, not where it went in. At least that's what Buck would do. But then, Buck knew nothing about prospecting.

The tracks had come from across the creek. Whoever had left them had approached the canyon from farther west. That's why Buck hadn't seen them before. If the man and burros had come from Cripple Creek they'd come in a roundabout way.

Hmm. Buck squatted on his boot heels and mulled it over. Suppose old Spooky had been headed back to his digs and stopped here for the night. If that was so, then his mine was in Shotgun Canyon somewhere. Unless he was just traveling through. But why had he come from the west? The other end of Shotgun Canyon was closer to Cripple Creek. Naw, it couldn't have been Spooky. It was some prospector who was just hunting and following his nose like a hound dog.

Damn. Standing, Buck shook his head. It had to have been some sourdough wandering around, looking for a place to pan or dig. He might have come from Canyon City or Pueblo. It wasn't Spooky. Spooky would have come from Cripple Creek and he would have known exactly where he was going. No, it wasn't Spooky Hallows. Unless—

"Whoa now," Buck said aloud. "What's this?" His fingers poked through the campfire ashes and picked up the quarter-inch remains of a tightly rolled cigarette. It had to have been thrown into the ashes after the fire had gone out. Spooky smoked cigarettes, and he smoked the ready-rolled ones. Most men chewed tobacco or smoked a pipe, and those who smoked cigarettes rolled their own. Buck had seen a few newcomers to Cripple Creek smoking the tailor-mades, but they were all Upper Tenners, not working men. At least one of the stores, trying to keep up with the latest fads from the east, was now stocking Duke's cigarettes. Spooky had camped here.

But why did he take a roundabout route to get here? To fool someone? If he thought someone was trailing him he sure wouldn't go directly to his digs.

"Aw hell," Buck said aloud. "I could worry about this all night. There's only one way to find out if Spooky done any diggin' in this canyon."

Walking back to his own camp, he studied the sky. The sun had gone down behind a range of mountains to the west. It reflected off the clouds hanging over the horizon, turning them a bright red. As Buck watched, the clouds changed colors and shapes. Within minutes, the red streaks had turned to blue — several shades of blue. The sky was growing dark.

It would take most of a day to ride down Shotgun Canyon. What was the old saying? A red sky at night is a sailor's delight. It didn't look like rain. Tomorrow would be a good time.

Sleeping was more difficult that night. The old wound in Buck's right hip wouldn't stop aching. He tried different positions, tried counting the tree tops, the ones he could see in the moonlight, tried to remember the words to an old song, and still couldn't sleep. In the hospital they had given him morphia a couple of times. For a moment Buck wished he had some, but on second thought he was still determined not to take any more of that stuff. A man could get hooked on morphia and it would rot his brains and drive him crazy.

He forced himself to concentrate on the words to the old song: The Camp Town race track . . . what was the rest of it? I'll bet my money on the bob-tailed nag, somebody bet on the bay.

Lord, lord.

It wasn't even his money that the robbers had been after. Lying awake, Buck recalled it all as if it had happened only yesterday. He'd gone into the bank in Canon City to deposit money from the sale of some cattle, and he was planning to ride up the

Shelf Road to Cripple Creek the next day. He had just stepped through the door, and his money was still in his pocket, when three gents with wild rags over their faces came in behind him and started shooting.

They fired two shots at the ceiling, and had everyone too scared to move. Dust and splinters rained down from the bullet holes. There were two men and a woman on Buck's side of the room, and three men behind the tellers' cages. "Open that safe," a masked man bellowed. "You," he pointed his pistol at a white-faced bank clerk wearing a celluloid collar, "Open it."

The heavy iron safe was as big as an outdoor privy, but the door wasn't locked. Without a word the young clerk took hold of the door handle with both hands and pulled it open. Buck was carrying his Peacemaker, but there were three of them. One pointed a double barreled shotgun at him and barked, "Shuck that pistol. Do it right now, mister, or your brains are gonna get scattered all over that wall."

It was useless to argue. Buck unbuckled his cartridge belt and let it fall, holster, pistol and all, to the floor. One gent was grabbing everything in the safe and stuffing it into a gunny sack while the other two kept their guns, a sixshooter and a shotgun, aimed at the customers and clerks. Buck stood still, making no threatening moves, hoping they wouldn't rob the customers.

The gent with the gunny sack tried to open an office door behind the tellers' cages, but it was locked from the inside. The bank bigshot wasn't about to stick his head out.

"Come on, get the rest of it and let's get the hell out of here."

"Stand still ever'body," yelled the man with the scattergun, "or I'll blast you to Kingdom Come."

The cash boxes in the tellers' cages were emptied into the sack, and the three were ready to leave. The one with the sack held it in one hand and a sixgun in the other. "Nobody moves. One move and we shoot." They backed toward the door, eyes on every man and woman in the room, guns leveled. Then came the holler from outside.

"You in there. This is the law. Come out with your hands up."

"Jesus Christ," a masked man swore.

"This is Sheriff Wilson speaking. We've got all the doors covered. You can't get away. Come out with your hands up."

"God damn it."

Buck was standing close to the door. His Peacemaker was at his feet. Could he, while the three gents were worried about the sheriff outside, reach down, grab the gun and plug a couple of them? He considered it. Naw. Let the sheriff do the shooting. That's what he was paid for.

"God damn it, let's run for it."

"Reckon how many're out there?"

"Maybe only one."

"Maybe a God damn army."

"Jumpin' Jesus Christ."

"I ain't goin' to no God damned prison. Let's run for it."

"No, wait a minute. I got an idea." The gent with a sixgun in his hand and nothing else grabbed the woman. Just wrapped one arm around her throat from behind, and yelled, "Tell that God damned sheriff we're gonna put a bullet in her head if he don't let us out of here."

The woman let out a strangled squawk and

71

started kicking and jumping. The arm tightened around her throat and the bore of a sixgun was pushed against her right temple. "Stand still, God damn it, or you're gonna die right here."

She stopped struggling and started pleading. "Let me go. Please. I've got two children. You can take my money. Let me go." She was middle-aged with plain square features and brown hair pulled back in a bun. Her long gray dress was without frills. A working class dress. "Please. Let me go."

"Hey, sheriff," the one with the scattergun yelled, "we got a woman in here with a gun at her head. You and ever'body else get back out of the way or we're gonna kill 'er. You got that?"

"You've got a woman?" The voice from outside sounded incredulous.

"You're God damned right, and she's gonna get a bullet in the head if we don't get out of here and on our horses. You got that."

"Let her go and come out with your hands up."

"Huh," snorted the one doing the yelling, "we're givin' the orders now. Drop your guns. Ever'body out there drop your guns and get back away from 'em. We're comin' out and if we don't get on our horses and get gone, this here woman's gonna die. You got that."

"Please," the woman begged. "Please. I've got two children. Let me go."

"Let her go," yelled the man outside.

"You don't think we'll kill 'er? I've got a gun at her head and my finger on the trigger. You shoot me and my finger'll pull the trigger before I die. Then she'll die. We're comin' out. If I see a gun in anybody's hand, I'll kill'er."

"Please let me go. Please."

They were at the door now, one man pushing the

72

woman ahead of him, an arm around her throat and a gun at her temple.

It was just bad luck that Buck happened to be standing near the door. His bad luck. If he had been on the other side of the room he would have done nothing. It wasn't his business. They probably would have let the woman go after they got out of town. For a few seconds, Buck wondered how that jasper could hold a gun at the woman's head while they got on their horses and got going. Put her on a horse in front of him? Drag her by the neck?

Either way, they probably wouldn't kill her.

Would they?

One of the masked men answered that question, "Sheriff, get back and stay back. When we get outside I'm gonna put a rope around her neck and tie it to the saddle horn. If you shoot me, the horse'll stampede and drag her to death. Stand back, now. We're comin' out."

She was going to be killed. Someone had to do something.

It was Buck's bad luck.

Chapter Nine

They were at the door, right in front of Buck Innes, ready to plunge outside. The woman was crying, begging. If he was going to do something he had to do it now.

Without a plan, without even thinking, he moved, moved as fast as he'd ever moved in his life. His right hand knocked the gun away from the woman's head and his left arm went around the gunman's throat. A shot was fired. Buck was dragging the man back, back and down. Then he was on the floor on his back with the man on top of him. The shotgun boomed. Men yelled. The woman screamed.

Gunfire. Yelling.

The man on top of Buck went limp. Buck had to get out from under him. He pushed, got the man off and rolled. His Peacemaker was on the floor. Buck reached for it. Something hit him in the right hind cheek. It felt like a sledge hammer blow. His whole lower body went numb.

A man yelled, "Don't shoot. Don't shoot."

"Put your hands up. Do it right now."

"Don't shoot."

It was quiet for a moment. Except for the woman's sobbing. Then a man's voice, a voice full of authority, said, "Everybody stand still. Stay right where you are. Stand still 'till we get this sorted out. Now then, how many are shot?"

Another man said, "Two of 'em are down. Only this one is still standing."

Buck tried to get up. He couldn't move his legs. He got his hands under his chest and tried to push himself up. Couldn't.

"Who's this one?"

"He's the one saved her."

"He did? How'd he do that?"

"He just grabbed one of 'em."

"He's been shot."

Hands were on him. He tried again to pick himself up. "Lie still, mister. Looks like you've got a bullet in you. We'll get a doctor."

Lie still? Hell, that's all he could do. He stayed down, hearing everything, but seeing only boots and the floor. A hand touched him gently on the cheek, and a woman said, "I sure do thank you, mister. I thank you and my husband and children thank you."

"Just lie still, mister. A doctor's comin'."

The doctor came. Buck raised his head and tried to see him. Couldn't. Efficient hands went over him. "Are you injured anywhere else?"

"Naw. I can't move my legs, is all." His voice sounded like someone else's.

Professional hands worked swiftly. Buck's pants were pulled down.

"All right. Bring a stretcher. We'll carry him to the clinic."

He waited. Waited with his bare ass sticking out.

He tried to pull his pants up. It was awkward.

"Lie still, sir. We'll have you in a bed in a few minutes."

"He saved my life."

"He saved the bank's money."

There was no pain. Just numbness. All Buck Innes could do was lie there on his belly with his bare ass shining at the ceiling.

What a place to get shot. But the doctor, a young man with a Prince Albert beard, thought that was a great place. It was the only place on Buck Innes's lean body where there was enough flesh to stop a bullet before it hit bone. The bullet had rammed itself in far enough to put some pressure on the end of the spine, but once it was removed the spine quickly got back to normal. Buck could again move his legs. But he couldn't turn over onto his back. For a week he lay on his stomach, then was able to shift to his left side. At least he could lie in two positions now. He'd never get over the embarrassment of having the doctor, a nurse and every damn body else come in and examine the wound.

Ten days after the shooting, the sheriff came for a visit. He was all smiles. "Two of those gunhands are dead and the other is in prison. We didn't have to take him far. The state prison is just over yonder. The woman you saved wanted to come in and thank you again, but the doctor said you weren't very sociable. Don't know as I blame you. I probably wouldn't want to see anyone either."

Buck was on his left side with two fat pillows under his head. "All I want to do, sheriff, is get back home. I've got a cow outfit to run and nobody to run it."

"You'll go home with some money in your pockets. The bank board asked me to give you this." Sheriff Wilson handed Buck a check for five hundred dollars. "You earned it. And don't worry about the doctor and hospital bills. The county is paying for it."

"Well now, that's mighty nice."

"And when you're able to walk, we're going to have a reception for you at the courthouse. Every man on the county board wants to shake your hand and so does the woman whose life you saved and her husband and kids."

Two days later Buck hobbled out of the one-story brick hospital, and before anyone knew he was gone he was on his way to Cripple Creek in a Concord coach pulled by six horses. He'd made arrangements with a neighbor to lead his saddle horse home. The two other passengers in the Concord thought it was strange the way he sat on one side with his knees drawn up, but when they tried to talk to him he only grunted. At home he holed up in the three-room house on the homesteads and didn't move any more than he had to. When he got on a horse again, two weeks later, he found he couldn't stand it for more than an hour. A month later he tried again. That time he lasted three hours. It was about then that the rich man from Denver offered him a good price for the homesteads. The location was excellent for a hunting lodge, the rich man said. After another month, Buck tried again to ride, and realized that he'd never again be able to sit on a horse all day without pain. Hired men rounded up his cattle and drove them to Canon City. The rich man's offer was accepted. Buck got a room at Mrs. Davenport's boarding house and allowed he'd stay there for the rest of his life. It would be a long time before he got on a horse again. If he ever did.

Now, a little over a year later, he'd been riding for most of three days, and boy did he feel it.

Daylight was a relief. He hobbled around, seeing to the horses, building a fire, cooking breakfast. As usual, he had to wake up Miss Hallows. He envied her, the way she could sleep.

"Up and at 'em," he said, trying to sound cheerful.

"Aw-wug." Her blond hair was tangled and her face was puffy with sleep. "If I don't get a bath pretty soon I won't be able to stand my own smell. God, how I hate sleeping in my clothes."

"Well, we only got chuck enough for a couple more days at the most, and then we'll have to go back."

Standing in her stocking feet, she rearranged her clothes, then reached down for her shoes. "What if we don't find my father before we run out of food? What will we do then?"

"There's lots of country we haven't seen. Reckon we'll have to go back to town and stock up on groceries and look some more." Buck glanced up at her and grinned. "Who knows, old Spooky, er Andy, might be in Cripple Creek now wondering where we are."

"What are your plans today?"

"Ride down Shotgun Canyon yonder. Somebody's been in there since the last hard rain and it might have been your dad."

"When was the last hard rain?"

"Who knows. I've seen lots of dark clouds over this way, but that don't mean much in this country." He turned the bacon slices over and put another stick of wood in the fire. "There's days when it's cloudy and dark all day and not a drop of rain falls. And there's times when one little cloud drifts overhead and dumps on you. Nobody can predict the weather in this country."

"How far is it down the canyon?"

"It'll take most of the day. If we don't see nobody we'll have to go back."

They were saddled up and on their way by sunup. As soon as they were in the canyon, the sun was out of sight, and the light was dim and gloomy. "I ain't been in here for a few years," Buck said, "but the last time I was the creek was easy to follow."

Burro tracks were plain to see in the soft dirt along the creek, and Buck knew they too were leaving tracks. There was nothing he could do about it. The narrow, sometimes invisible, trail wound around granite boulders as big as a horse, and the stream gurgled happily downhill to the mighty Arkansas. The horses had no trouble stepping around the boulders. A mile into the canyon, both sides rose straight up. Cracks in the rock walls ran in all directions and some of the cracks were filled with other minerals, once molten. The variety of minerals created colorful streaks in the walls.

The girl hung onto her saddle horn and took it all in, her head tilted so she could see the top. The horses' backs dipped and swayed. Twice they crossed the creek to get to better footing. A few more miles, and they came to a narrow pocket where tall grass grew. On their right, the canyon rose straight up, but on their left the hill could be climbed by a man on foot who could grab handholds. A horse would never make it. Buck reined up and studied the terrain.

"Yup," he said aloud. "Whoever he was, he stopped here for a while. Some of the grass has been cropped off by the burros."

"Whoever who was?"

There was no doubt in Buck's mind, by now. He'd been thinking about that cigarette butt back near the other end of the canyon, and here was another. It had been mashed flat by a boot heel.

He recalled how Spooky Hallows had tried to get him interested in cigarettes. Buck had chewed tobacco once as a youngster. It had made him sick. He'd tried smoking a pipe, but couldn't keep the damn thing lighted. Years later, his friend showed him how to roll a cigarette, but the first time he tried one hot ashes fell off the end of it and burned a hole in his best wool shirt. He'd given up on tobacco.

But smoking those ready-rolled cigarettes was Spooky's one extravagance.

"It was your dad," he said matter-of-factly.

"We're going to find him now, aren't we, Mr. Innes?"

"Don't know. But we've found where he's been."

On they went, winding around boulders, crossing and recrossing the stream. The sun finally climbed high enough to shine down into the canyon, then a cloud drifted under the sun and it was dark and gloomy again. About noon they passed under a stack of huge boulders, a place that had always made Buck uncomfortable. It seemed that nothing was holding the boulders on the side of the hill, and any little disturbance could start them rolling down into the canyon bottom. As before, he reminded himself that those rocks had been there a thousand years or longer and they weren't going to break loose today. But he couldn't help thinking about the destruction they would cause if they did break loose.

Why, they would dam up the creek, causing it to change course, and the creek would wash out the side of the hill, causing a rock slide and, hell, in another thousand years it would dig out another canyon. And someday they would break loose. Maybe next year, maybe in a thousand years, but someday.

Buck was always glad to get past those rocks.

"Aren't we going to stop for lunch?"

"Yeah. I recollect another little pocket ahead and we'll stop there and let the horses rest."

The sun was out again, and its light and warmth were more than welcome. The temperature warmed up a good ten degrees when the sun came out. Then they were at the next pocket. A good place to stop except for one thing: there was no place for Buck to hide from her while he drained his bladder. He unloaded the pack horse, offsaddled her horse then got back on his bay.

"I'm goin' on downstream a ways, Miss Hallows, to see what's ahead. You wait here."

Whew. What a relief it was to get around a bend in the stream, out of her sight. How in hell did she hold it back?

In less than an hour they were horseback again, riding along the creek, crossing the creek, around a bend, looking up at sheer cliffs of seamed and cracked metamorphic rock. They rode across a wide place on the trail where their horses walked on solid granite. Stunted oak and chokeberry bushes grew out of cracks in the granite. The sky was clear, but the sun was past its zenith, out of sight. Its light could be seen along the top of the north cliff.

A groan prompted Buck to look back at the girl. She was hanging onto the saddle horn and wore a pained expression on her face. "Oh-h-h. I can't stay on this horse another minute. Can't we walk a while?"

Buck was uncomfortable himself, and he silently agreed that walking would relieve the ache in his right hip. But he said, "It ain't much farther. Can't be much farther. We'll be out of this canyon in a couple of hours." He kicked his horse on with spurless boot heels. They went around more giant boulders, and he reined up.

Damn.

A rock slide, sure enough. Thousands of years of rain, hail and snowmelt had caused the rock wall to sheer off at the top and come rolling down in a million pieces. It had formed a dam across the stream, and the water had backed up into a deep pool before it found a way around the rocks. The slide had to have happened in the past few years. That made Buck realize that the canyon was always changing. It would change again and it could happen any time.

How to get around it? On one side of the creek, the canyon went almost straight up. On the other side the hill sloped steeply. Could a horse walk on the side of the hill and get around the slide? Going on a few steps, Buck saw where burros had walked around it. But burros were better in the rocks than horses. They could get around like a goat.

It would be risky. Maybe this was a time to walk and lead the horses. No, he'd be damned if he'd do that. He'd always said he wouldn't go where a horse couldn't carry him. Well, there were two things he could do, he could go on and risk a fall and get himself and the horses hurt, or he could get down, throw rocks and clear a path. If he got hurt, there was no one to help him. The girl wouldn't be any help. No, it would be foolish to take a risk he didn't have to.

Buck dismounted and started picking up rocks and throwing them downhill. Looking back at the girl, he wanted to yell at her to, for Pete's sake, get down and help, but, aw hell, what was the use. He worked for nearly an hour making a path through the rocks where a horse could walk. The footing still wasn't good, but he'd ridden over worse places.

"Do you think it's safe now, Mr. Innes?"

Straightening his back with a grunt, he said, "If you want to, right here's a good place to walk and lead your horse. This is gonna be a little bit tricky." He watched her dismount sorely, then he stepped into the saddle and kicked his horse in the sides.

The bay horse took a few steps, stopped, tried to turn back, then, with its nose down, went on, stepping carefully. Now Buck was hanging onto the saddle horn, his feet out of the stirrups, ready to throw himself off away from the horse where it wouldn't roll over him if it fell.

One step at a time. Buck held the pack horse's lead rope in his hand, not wanting it to pull on the saddle if it balked. He rode stiffly, afraid to look back. A shift of his weight in the saddle could throw the horse off balance enough that it would lose its footing. Walking slowly, carefully, the bay horse climbed two steps, went down two steps, over a rock, over the trunk of a small dead aspen. "Take your time, feller," Buck said, quietly. "Just stay right side up." A few more steps, and the horse stopped. "I know what you're thinkin'," Buck said, "but look at it this way, we can't turn around. Unless you want to walk backwards, we got to keep goin'."

"Is anything the matter?" the girl said.

"Nope. Nothin'." He urged the horse on.

And finally they were on the other side of the rock slide.

When he got to good footing again, Buck looked back. The pack horse was right behind him. The girl was far behind, moving cautiously, leading her horse. Buck scratched the bay's neck. "You're one damn good horse, feller. Good thing you was born and raised in the mountains. You've got a hell of a lot more sense than I have."

Then the girl and her horse were across too. "My God, I didn't think a horse could do that. How did they keep from slipping?"

"They don't want to fall any more than we want 'em to," Buck said. But he knew it would have been easier and safer to walk and lead the horses the way she did. It would have been safer for him and the horses too. Only a cattleman's pride had kept him horseback. It was the kind of foolish pride that could get a man hurt.

"Get on your horse again and let's go," he said to the girl. "I ain't gonna feel right 'till we get out of this canyon and in the sun."

A half-hour later—past mid-afternoon—they saw the mine.

Chapter Ten

It was in another pocket, a spot where a spring seeped up through the ground and joined the creek. Buck remembered stopping here before, years ago, driving cattle from the Arkansas River which wasn't more than ten miles east. It was a good grassy spot where horses could graze and a man could rest. The mine wasn't here then. Reining up, Buck took a long careful look. He saw nothing human or animal. But someone had been here. Flat rocks were laid out for cooking with a rock ring around them. Black wood ashes covered most of the flat rocks. The ashes had been rained on. Buck didn't know when it had rained last in Shotgun Canyon, but it wasn't long ago. Two empty tin cans lay in the grass. The grass had been cropped by grazing animals, and burro droppings were plentiful. Plentiful, but not fresh. An empty wooden box stood on end near the camp ashes. Painted on it in red letters were the words:
GIANT POWDER No. 3 DANGER
That's what it took — a whole box of dynamite — to blast out the far end of the pocket where the

granite wall was almost perpendicular. Whoever did it had used a single jack drill and a sledge hammer to punch holes in the wall for the sticks of dynamite. And he'd done some digging with a pick and shovel too. He'd blasted and dug a cave in the wall. It wasn't a deep cave. It was only about three feet into the wall. But it was a sure enough man-made cave.

This was a mine. It had to be Spooky's mine. But where was Spooky?

And where were the tools? Buck's eyes took in everything in sight. There were no digging tools. Strange.

"Is this it? Did we find it?"

"Yeah," Buck said, dismounting slowly. "This is her."

"Where is my father?"

"That's a puzzler. He's been here sometime within the last month or so. He took some ore out of that hole and left. I'll bet he took it right straight to the mill. He could be in Cripple Creek right now."

"Wouldn't our paths have crossed if he was going back while we were coming here?"

"Naw. If I'd known this mine was here—if I wasn't lookin'—I'd of come a different way. I'd of come . . ." Buck stopped talking in midsentence. Spooky had come far out of his way to get here. He was trying to throw someone off his trail. No, that didn't make sense. He left too good a trail.

"Now this," he said to the girl, "is a puzzler."

"It's a real gold mine, isn't it?"

"Yeah, that's what she is."

"Then I, we, have to get back to town and file a claim on it."

Buck dropped his reins and walked. He walked

86

in all directions, looked in the cave, examined the shattered rock that had been blasted and shoveled out and piled in front of it, studied the cliff and the hill surrounding the pocket, walked down the creak, and came back to the girl. "I don't see no markers. Nobody's claimed her."

She climbed awkwardly off her horse. "Then let's go back to Cripple Creek and do whatever is necessary to claim it."

"Don't you want to find your dad?"

"Of course, but as you said, he's probably in Cripple Creek with a load of ore."

Buck mulled that over. He had said it, but he wasn't sure he believed it. This was a mine. Someone had been working like a slave taking ore out of here. There were no markers, an indication that nobody had staked a claim on it. Spooky hadn't filed a claim. This was exactly what Buck had looked for since he started looking for Spooky. Spooky was either back in Cripple Creek or he'd got hurt on his way back.

But he'd been missing for about three weeks. If he was hurt, he'd have died by now. A man could go a long time without eating, but not very long without water. The old sourdough was dead. The best Buck could hope for was to find his friend's remains.

Spooky's daughter was impatient. "What are we going to do?"

Buck walked over to her, sat on a boulder and said, "Here's the story," and he told her what had been going through his mind.

"You really believe my father is dead?"

"I'm not sure about anything, but that's the only thing that makes sense. I'm sorry to have to tell you, but I think you ought to expect the worst."

"You don't think he could be in Cripple Creek now?"

"Naw. He's been missin' too long."

"Then what are we going to do?"

"Go back. Take the shortest way back like Spooky would. See if we can find his body and his burros."

"What about this mine?"

"What about it?"

"If it was my father's, then I should claim it."

"Hmm." This was something else to think about. She was right. No use leaving it for somebody else to take over. She was no miner, but maybe she could sell the claim. Yeah, she could probably do that. And, when he thought about it, no use leaving it for those yahoos who'd been following them. "All right," he said, finally, "let's put up some markers."

"How do we do that?"

Groping inside his shirt pockets, Buck found a stub of a wooden pencil. He lifted his belt knife out of its sheath and began whittling a point on the pencil. "We'll use some of that paper Mrs. Davenport wrapped the bread in." The pencil sharpened, he took a half-loaf of bread out of a pack pannier and unwrapped it. Handing the paper to her, he said, "Here, you can do the writin'."

"What shall I write?"

"I don't know." Buck's face screwed up in thought as he tried to recall some of the mining claims he'd seen in writing. Then he dictated: "Somethin' like, 'I, Anita Hallows, do hereby lay claim to twenty acres of valuable minerals around a pocket in the southerly end of Shotgun Canyon in El Paso County of Colorado.' Write that four times, one for each corner."

While she stood beside her horse and used the seat of the saddle for a desk, he picked up the 30-30 and walked back to the creek. More questions went through his mind. Would they bring their horses around the rock slide as he and the girl had done, walk and lead them, or did they know their way around to the other end of Shotgun Canyon? If they did, would they come that way? When would they catch up? A glance at the shadows on the south end of the canyon told him the day was getting on. They wouldn't catch up today, but tomorrow, probably about mid-morning, they'd be here. He and the girl should be on their way back to Cripple Creek by then. And what would they do if they caught up?

Now, that was a dumb question. Buck knew what they would do.

He wanted out of the canyon. This was no place to be trapped. Put up those markers and get the hell out. Get back to town and file a claim before those yahoos could.

Working fast, he gathered rocks and made a foot-high pile near the creek on one side of the pocket, then on the other side. "This ain't twenty acres," he said to the girl when she came up to him, "but the best part is on top."

He placed a handwritten note inside each pile of rocks, then went back to the horses.

"Where are we going now?"

Nodding at the top of the canyon wall, he said, "Up there. If this is turned into a big mine, up there's where most of the diggin'll take place. At least I think it will. But I'm no miner. Anyway, up there is where we need to stake a claim."

"Can we do it before dark?"

"I think so. It's only about a mile, maybe less,

out of this here ditch and it won't take long to plant those notes. I wish this mine was on the other side, on the east side. Then we'd be on our way back to town."

"We have to go east?"

"Yeah, but not 'till we plant some markers on the west side. That means ridin' some miles out of our way."

"All right. We don't need to do anything more here, then?"

"Well, it might help if we could find some high grade ore to take back with us, but I wouldn't know the stuff if I saw it."

"Yes, that would help, wouldn't it."

"Yep. But you can bet old Spooky, er, Andy has already picked up anything valuable that was layin' here to be picked up. And I ain't about to go diggin' for more. Besides," Buck took another long look around, "I don't want to stay in here tonight."

"Why?"

Instead of answering, he got on his horse, picked up the pack horse's lead rope and rode out of the pocket. Before he started to boot the bay saddle horse across the creek, he looked back and saw she was climbing on her horse.

The canyon walls rose straight up again and huge boulders at the bottom forced the creek to wind around them. In places the horses had to stay in the creek, and search for footing in its bottom. Then, finally, the canyon floor sloped down and so did the walls. Within a half-mile, Buck could look up and see the southern horizon. In another half-mile they were out of the canyon among some rolling, treeless hills. The stream drifted along, splashing white foam against some of the boulders.

By then the sun was sitting on the Continental Divide.

"Boy, oh boy," the girl said, "am I ever glad to get out of there."

"Yeah."

"Did you say Cripple Creek is east of here?"

"East and a little north."

"But we have to go west to get above the mine?"

"Yep."

"How far is Cripple Creek?"

"A good two days ride."

"Then we'll have to camp around here somewhere?"

"Yep."

They had to double back and climb to the west side of the canyon, and just before dark they came to a patch of scrub oak that Buck had picked out as a landmark. From up here the country rolled away to the east and the Arkansas Valley. Dismounting, Buck pushed his way through the several acres of thick brush and walked as close to the rim of the canyon as he dared. When he looked down he could see that they were above the mine. This was the place to put up some markers.

Miss Hallows had dismounted too. "Are we going to stay here tonight?"

"Yep. It's gettin' too dark to do anything else. I've got to get these horses hobbled while I can see to do it."

"Are we going to have a camp fire?"

"Naw. Not tonight. We'll eat a cold supper."

"Why?"

"Well, uh . . ." He didn't want to tell her and he didn't answer.

"Mr. Innes?"

"Huh?"

"Are you going to tell anyone about my father's mine when we get back?"

"Aw, I don't know. I reckon not. It'd start a stampede."

"Would you wait until I get everything in order? I mean, until I can make some arrangements for the mine?"

"Yeah, if that's what you want."

"Will you promise?"

Turning to her he snapped, "I said I would, didn't I?"

She looked down. "Yes. I'm sorry."

Horses hobbled and grazing, he fumbled in the pack panniers until he found two tins of dried beef. He wished they'd taken a good long drink of water out of the stream before they rode up here, but he hadn't thought of it at the time. They'd just have to be thirsty until morning when they'd cross the creek again on their way back to town. While he opened cans, Buck hummed and sang, barely audible, "Camp Town race track five miles long.

"Here," he said, handing the girl a tin of beef. "Eat out of the can quick before the air can taint it." Then he resumed singing, mostly under his breath, "Doo-dah, doo-dah."

"Don't you know any other songs?"

"Sure, I know lots of songs?"

"Why don't you sing something else?"

" 'Cause I only know one tune."

"Have we got any water?"

"Nope." At that, Buck carried his bed away from hers, sat on it, ate his tin of beef, walked farther into the dark, relieved himself, went back to his bed, pulled off his boots and crawled between the blankets.

Lying on his back, hands under his head, looking up at the stars, he heard the girl moving about. Heard her unroll her sleeping bag, heard her footsteps in the grass as she walked away in the opposite direction, and heard her coming back.

"Mr. Innes?"

"Yeah."

"It's so dark I can't find my bed."

"Sounds like you're too far east. Be careful or you'll fall off the world."

"Oh my God." Her voice was filled with fear. "Wh—which way do I go?"

"Aw, don't worry. There's four acres of scrubs between you and the canyon. Turn west. That's left. You'll find it."

Heard her slow, careful footsteps, heard her groan as she stumbled, and finally heard the rustle of a heavy quilt.

"Mr. Innes?"

"Huh?"

"What keeps the horses from falling off?"

"They can see. A horse can find his way in the dark where a man couldn't find his a—his nose with both hands."

"Oh. We'll be back in Cripple Creek in two days?"

"Ought to."

"Boy oh boy, will I be glad to get back."

Yeah, Buck said under his breath, shifting onto his left side, trying to ease the ache in his right hip. Me too.

At first light he was up, pulling on his boots. The air was so clear it sparkled. But chilly. Shivering, walking with a limp the first fifty steps, he saw to the horses, then gathered rocks. At first he

93

tried to carry the 30-30, keep it handy, but he couldn't carry it and rocks too. He made two foot-high piles about a half-mile apart and a good distance from the buck brush where they could easily be seen. He put one of the girl's notes in each pile. That was the most walking he'd done in years, but it did relieve the pain in his hip. "Doo-dah, doo-dah."

Dark clouds were gathering over the Continental Divide, but the eastern sky was still clear.

The girl was up when he walked back to the saddles and pack panniers. They ate the rest of the bread and two cans of fruit. He was going after the horses when he saw the men coming.

There were three of them. On horseback. With rifles.

Chapter Eleven

Running wasn't something Buck Innes liked to do, but he broke into a shuffling, stiff-legged run now, trying to get to the horses. Looking back over his shoulder, he saw the men riding at a gallop. They were coming from the south, from the mouth of Shotgun Canyon. He'd never make it to the horses, get the hobbles off, get them saddled. He changed directions and ran the best he could to the saddles and pack panniers.

Just as he grabbed the 30-30, the first shot was fired.

Buck heard the lead slug whistle past his head, and he hit the ground on his belly behind the saddles. Without taking aim, he fired a shot in the direction of the men, hoping it would stop them. It worked for a few seconds. No longer.

When he looked over the saddles, Buck saw them dismount, then walk carefully toward him. One threw his rifle to his shoulder. Buck ducked so fast he tasted dirt as the bullet went over his head.

They had him. There were three of them and

they were fanned out. If he was lucky, he might throw a shot and hit one, but the other two would make a sieve out of him. God damn. Glancing at the girl, he saw her just standing there with her mouth open. He yelled, "Hit the ground, woman. Get down." She didn't hear him.

Buck put down the 30-30 and yanked the Colt Peacemaker out of its holster, thumbing the hammer back at the same instant. It would take at least a second to aim and fire a rifle. A pistol wasn't as accurate, but it was a hell of a lot faster. Quickly, he raised his head and gun hand and fired at the nearest man, a man who was aiming a rifle at him. The man immediately lowered the rifle and dropped to his knees. But he wasn't hit, only scared. Buck could see that. Then two rapid shots from the other men thudded into the saddles and pinged off the ground near Buck's legs.

He was as good as dead. So was Spooky's daughter. The three, whoever they were, had what they wanted, Spooky's mine and nobody alive to say it wasn't theirs. Or they soon would have.

Well hell, Buck Innes, he muttered to himself, what're you gonna do, just lie here and let them kill you. Shoot. Shoot as fast as you can cock the hammer and pull the trigger. Hit at least one of them. Make them pay. "Doo-dah."

Jumping to his feet, he faced them for a moment, firing, holding the trigger back and fanning the hammer with his left hand. He fired until the firing pin hit an empty shell, then he turned and ran. He ran, bent low, heading for the thick buck brush. A bullet plucked at his shirt tail. Another knocked his hat off. As fast as his stiff old legs could carry him, he ran, then dove head first into the brush, rolling. While bullets clipped twigs off

96

the brush, he got to his hands and knees and scrambled on until he came to a shallow gulley.

He stumbled and rolled again, coming to a stop face down in the gulley. For a few seconds he lay there and tried to get his wind. Then he heard them coming, yelling:

"He can't be far. Find the sonofabitch."

"He's gotta be hit. I couldn't miss that many times."

"You can't see twenty feet in here."

"Got to find the Goddamned old fart."

They'd find him. Sooner or later they'd find him. But — and then it occurred to Buck — he was in a good spot in this gulley. He was a poor target. And he wasn't hit. He looked himself over. No blood. No pain. Even his right hip wasn't hurting now. All right, you bunch of blood-suckers, I can hear you and see you comin'. You won't see me 'till it's too late. Come on, get close enough and I'll pick you off one at a time.

He waited. They pushed through the brush, coming closer. Get ready. Then, aw hell, you dumb old bat, your gun is empty. Reload, you stupid old turkey. Fingers moving as fast as he could move them, Buck pinched out the empty .45 cartridges and reloaded with cartridges he took from his gun belt. Then he was ready. Come on. Show yourselves.

But they didn't come.

"He's in here somewhere." — "Got to be. Can't be far away." — "Yeah, but he ain't movin', and we are. He knows where we are and we don't know where he is."

Grinning, Buck said to himself, now ain't that a cryin' shame.

All movement stopped.

"What the hell're we gonna do?"

"We got to get 'im, that's for sure."

"What about the girl?"

"Don't worry about her. She ain't goin' no-where."

Maybe, Buck thought, she'll be smart enough to get on one of their horses and ride like hell. She knew which way to go. He hoped she did. While the three gunsels were beating the scrubs looking for him, maybe she could get away. If she didn't . . . ? Buck felt as if he was abandoning her, leaving her at the mercy of three killers. He couldn't do that to Spooky's daughter. But then he couldn't help her if he was dead. And he'd sure as hell be dead if he ran out of the scrubs and tried to . . . what? What could he do?

Could he, by Indianing his way through the brush, get out while the killers were in it, and get himself and the girl on their horses? He'd done his share of Indianing through the timber and brush when he was hunting meat. With luck he might do it. He had to try.

Slowly, carefully, he crawled out of the gulley. Crawled on his belly, stopping every few feet to listen. He could hear footsteps off to his right. A happy thought came to his mind: if they didn't know where one another was, they might get trigger happy and shoot at the sound of somebody moving.

"Jesus Christ, I can't see ten feet ahead of me."

"Shit, there ain't more'n a couple of acres of this stuff. Keep lookin'."

On his hands and knees now, Buck moved, watching where he put each hand, each knee. Moved cautiously. Stopped, listened. The three gunmen had stopped too. They were listening.

Now it was a waiting game. He couldn't move until they moved. He couldn't make a sound until they made a sound to drown out his sound.

The sun came up and brought more light. That was bad news. Buck was easier to see now. Then, as quick as it had showed itself, the sun went behind a cloud again.

One of the three moved. "Hey, I'm over here. Don't shoot 'till you see the sonofabitch."

"Wish that Goddamned sun would stay out. Wouldn't you know it'd be cloudy today."

Two men were moving. Buck moved. Moved on his hands and knees. Carefully. Finally, he could see through the scrubs and see the horses. Flat on his belly, he let his eyes rove over everything. Three saddled horses were off to the south, standing with their reins on the ground. The girl was near them, standing humped over, looking like a whipped, helpless puppy. Buck listened. No one was moving. How to do it?

If the horses stayed where they were, he could maybe get over there and keep a horse between him and the scrubs. They wouldn't shoot one of their own horses. If the girl would move fast and did as he told her, maybe they could get horseback before the three gunsels got wise.

If. That word again.

All right, a sorrel was the closest. He'd leave that one and go to the brown horse and the bay on the other side of it.

He listened. No movement. Plan it carefully, he told himself. Know exactly what you're going to do before you move. He wished the girl would look his way so he could give her some kind of signal. The terrain south of the scrubs was fairly flat to the end of the canyon, then it changed to hilly. Get horseback and get in those hills as fast as the horses could run. Once in the hills they wouldn't be good targets. Until then . . . There was a grassy draw between him and the hills. A man could lie in the draw and be out of sight. The draw ran north and south, paralleling the canyon. A man on foot could crawl the length of it and get into the hills, while a man on a horse would stick up like a bullseye on a paper target.

Yet Buck and Miss Hallows had to get on those horses. That was the only way. All right, no use Indianing now. He'd be in the open. Had to run. Run like hell.

"Doo-dah."

Buck Innes crawled to the edge of the brush, took a careful look around, then jumped up and ran. As he ran, stiff-legged, he motioned to the girl, trying to tell her without yelling to get on a horse. She stood still, staring at him. Running as best he could, Buck got on the other side of the sorrel before he heard a holler behind him. Now he was seen.

"Miss Hallows," he yelled, "get on a horse. Hurry up." He was gasping for breath when he got to her. "Come on, get on that one." He pointed to the brown horse. She stood still.

"Come on, God damn it. Get on that horse." He grabbed her arms, roughly, shook her. "Move, God damn it."

She was frozen with fear. Her mouth opened but no sound came out. He pushed her toward the brown horse. She stumbled and fell. "Get up. Come on." She stayed on her hands and knees.

Bullets were flying over Buck's head. A glance back showed him the sorrel horse was between him and the scrubs. Two of the men had come out of the scrubs and were firing, but over his head.

For the first time in a hell of a lot of years, Buck pleaded, trying to keep his voice calm, talking like a father to a child, "Please, Miss Hallows, we've got to get on these horses and ride. Those men are trying to kill us."

A bullet pinged off the saddle on the sorrel horse. Startled, the horse jumped, ran a few steps, stopped. It was no longer a shield. Buck was in the open where a man with a rifle couldn't miss.

He yanked the Colt .45 out of its holster and fired back, fired hastily. Now the three of them were out of the brush. Buck had no chance. Again he ran. He put his head down and willed his legs to move faster. Ran toward the grassy draw. Lead slugs sang a deadly song around him, thudded into the ground, screamed off a rock. At the draw he dove into it headfirst like a man diving into shallow water, hanging onto the Colt. His breath was knocked out of his lungs with a "Whoosh" when he landed.

Rolling onto his back, he tried to get up, fell back, tried again. He had to get up, at least to his knees. Had to shoot back. If he didn't they would run up and pump lead into him.

Ordering himself to move, he got to his knees, aimed the Colt in the direction of the men and fired. They stopped. It came to Buck in a flash that these men were not gunfighters. They liked to shoot, but they didn't like to be shot at. When lead flew their way, they ducked, That was the only reason Buck was still alive. For the moment, he had the advantage. At least they thought he did. He wasn't so sure. They were in the open but far enough away that he would have to take careful aim to hit one with a sidearm. He had to move again. They knew where he was, and they would soon spread out and come at him from different directions. They might stay out of pistol range, but they'd come. He moved.

Bending low, as low as he could, he ran again. He ran around a curve in the draw, stopped and looked back. They'd seen him, seen the top of his head or something. They were running, trying to get into a position to shoot. There was no time to take aim. Buck snapped another shot, hoping to slow them down, make them cautious. Two of them pulled up immediately. Brave men they were not. But the third one was on the other side of the draw and still coming. He was moving cautiously, trying to work his way to where he could get a shot.

He had to be stopped too, and there was only one way to do it. Buck raised his head and gun hand above the draw, squinted down the short barrel and squeezed the trigger. The man was bending low and walking right at him. Then he fell onto his stomach. A bullet from behind thudded into the dirt near Buck's head, causing him to jerk his head down. He didn't know whether he'd hit the man or just scared him. He had to run again.

The fault in the earth that Buck was in zigzagged toward the hills, toward the end of Shotgun Canyon, and Buck was headed in that direction. At least two men with rifles were running after him, trying to get a shot at him. If he could get to the hills maybe he could find something to fort up behind. There should be some boulders, an arroyo, or something.

He ran until he thought his legs were going to collapse from under him. Rifle shots followed him.

Finally he was between two hills. But that was

worse than being in the open. There were no trees, no boulders, no nothing. The gunmen could get on top of the hills and shoot down at him. That's what they'd do too. Buck had to keep running. He turned north and ran into the mouth of the canyon.

Heart pounding, lungs pumping, legs wobbly, Buck ran. A lead slug screamed off a horse-sized granite boulder. Ducking behind the boulder, Buck stopped and tried to get his breathing back to normal. He thought his heart was going to jump out of his chest. His hand holding the Colt was shaking. He holstered the Colt. For the moment he was safe. He was forted up. Anyone coming at him would be hard to miss, even with a pistol. Gradually, Buck's lungs slowed their pumping. Gradually his heart slowed its beating.

Where was his hat? Oh yeah, it had been shot right off his head up there on the rim. He missed his hat. Never, for as long as he could remember, had he ever gone outdoors without a hat. Not having a hat made him feel exposed, naked.

A bullet ricocheted off the top of the boulder and went whanging away up the canyon. Another. Let them shoot. Buck was getting used to hearing slugs whining around him. Hell, he'd made it this far. By some miracle he'd survived a hell of a lot of gunfire. They weren't going to hit him now.

Instead of looking over the top of the boulder, he got down and looked out from along the bottom. They were standing there in the mouth of the canyon, too far for a pistol shot. Two of them.

Only two of them. That brought a grin to Buck's face. He'd hit that sonofabitch up there. The odds were better now. In fact, if he had that 30-30 he might even drive them away.

But as it was—the grin vanished from Buck's face—it was a standoff. He was trapped in the canyon. They couldn't come in after him and he couldn't get out.

Looking around, he saw that the canyon wall on the west was sheer rock, and on the east a rocky hill rose steep enough that a man would have to climb hand over hand to get to the top of it. He'd be a perfect target while he was doing that. The riflemen would have a lot of fun shooting him down. No, it couldn't be done. Not in the daylight. Maybe in the dark.

Wait for dark? Hell, Buck mused, what else can I do?

Lying on his belly where he could peer around the bottom edge of the boulder, Buck waited.

But not for long.

With a sickening WHANG, a rifle bullet hit a rock near Buck's head. Pieces of the rock stung his face. He said aloud, "What the holy, humped up hell?"

Rolling onto his back he immediately saw where the shot had come from. A rifleman was standing in the edge of the buckbrush on top of the western rim, aiming down at him. He saw a puff of smoke come from the rifle barrel.

Chapter Twelve

Buck Innes threw himself to one side and rolled. He heard the slug hit the ground where he'd been. He crawled on his feet and hands like a four-legged spider to the opposite side of the boulder. The man on the rim couldn't hit him here, but the two out in front could. Two out in front? Buck swore. Yep. Two out there and one on top. He'd missed the man he thought he'd hit up there.

"God damn it," he said aloud. "No. I take that back. Excuse me, Lord."

Move. Run some more. Deeper into the canyon, Buck ran. He dodged rocks and boulders, splashed across the creek, heard bullets smack into the ground near him, heard them whine over his head. Glancing up, he could see the man on top running too, pushing through the brush, trying to keep up with him, looking for a shot. All Buck could do was run and hope to find another fort, one that protected him from all directions. With all the rocks and boulders on the floor of the canyon he ought to find something—if he didn't get hit first. Deeper into the canyon he went, out of breath, stumbling now from weakness. He had to find a fortress soon.

He couldn't run anymore. He was like a wounded elk that had run as far as it could and would have to give up and die. His vision was blurring, his head spinning. He wasn't going to die from a bullet wound, he was going to die from a heart burst.

Staggering, he went on, fell, got up, staggered a few more steps and collapsed.

All he could do was lie there on his left side and gasp for breath. His legs were numb, his hands were trembling. He gasped, coughed, gasped some more. Where in this damned canyon was he? Where were the gunmen? Forcing himself, neck muscles straining, he raised his head. At first he saw nobody. Then the gunsel on top appeared, put a rifle to his shoulder.

Buck didn't have the strength to move. Shoot, his mind said. Shoot and be done with it. A man could run only so far. If the Almighty had intended for men to run, He would have given them four legs.

The old song went through his mind again: Camp Town race track . . . Suddenly a realization came to him.

He was right in front of Spooky's mine.

Get in there, Buck Innes, he said to himself. Get inside that man-made cave. Get your old bones up and get to hell in there. Summoning more strength then he knew he had, he got up, staggered, ran, stumbled, staggered and ran across the creek and into the cave. Bullets followed him, but he didn't even hear them.

He had to go around the mine dump, the pile of shattered rocks, to get inside the cave, but it occurred to him that the man on top would have to shoot straight down to hit him, and maybe he wouldn't want to get that close to the edge. Then he was inside the cave, behind the pile of rocks.

Again he collapsed, gasping, lungs pumping. But now he could grin again. He was safe. No way could they shoot him out of here. He had the roof of the cave over his head and a pile of rocks in front of him. What more could a man ask for?

Only he wished his heart would slow down. It sounded like one of the steam-powered air pumps they used in the mines. Whump, whump, whump.

Slowly, he raised up and looked over the pile of rocks. A man stood on the other side of the creek, holding a rifle, looking in Buck's direction. It was no one Buck had ever seen before today. He was joined by a second man. One pointed at him, looked up at the man on the rim, and pointed again. He raised his rifle and fired a shot. The slug sang harmlessly off the rocks.

Buck lifted the Peacemaker out of its holster and thumbed the hammer back. "Come a little closer, you sonsofbitches. I dare you. Just come across the creek."

Whump, whump, went his heart. His face was hot, while the top of his head was cold. Sweat had the blue cotton shirt stuck to his body. The air around him was hot, humid and sticky. A cool breeze would have felt mighty good.

But still he grinned. He could stay here as long as they could. They didn't have Spooky's mine, he did. Thinking of Spooky reminded him of Spooky's daughter. She was up there at the mercy of three killers. Unless she finally got smart, jumped on a horse and headed for town as fast as the horse could run. She had the opportunity. All three of the gunsels were after Buck. She could get away. Sure, she probably did. She was probably headed on a high lope for Cripple Creek right now. She knew which direction to go. All she had to do was ride east, cross the creek and keep going. If she missed the town she'd come to a road — either the Shelf Road south of town or the Florissant Road to the north.

Anyway he'd done the best he could for her. Spooky, he said in his mind, wherever you are, I hope you know that.

The men across the creek had drawn back out of sight. And the cool breeze he'd been wishing for came. It was good. It made him feel better. His lungs and heart had slowed to normal. Oh, the Camp Town . . .

With the breeze came a few drops of rain. Big fat drops. Buck looked up at what he could see of the sky. The sky was darker than Old Coalie's ass. More drops fell. Faster now.

And suddenly the bottom fell out of the sky.

It started as hail. Hailstones the size of pigeon eggs pounded the earth, bounced off the boulders and set up a roar like a tornado. Above the roar, Buck could hear the boom of thunder. Lightning split the sky. He had a good shelter inside the cave, and he was glad he wasn't out there somewhere on a horse. Any horse would get nervous at being pounded like that. A man on a horse not only took a beating from hail, he had a nervous, jumpy mount on his hands too. It hailed a lot in the Colorado mountains. There'd been times when Buck had had to get down, offsaddle his horse and put the saddle blanket over his head and shoulders. All he could do for the horse was hang onto him. Now he had a cave.

And — Buck grinned again — those gunsels with the rifles were out in it. Ain't that a shame. But then, so was Spooky's daughter. Dammit. Why in hell did she have to come along, anyway? Doesn't matter why, he told himself, she was up there and he had to do something for her.

He'd wait until dark and see if he could sneak up on their camp. If she was still alive and still there, he could maybe come up in the dark, cut her loose and catch a couple of horses. It wouldn't be easy. The three gunsels would keep one man awake and on guard. It might be impossible.

It was the only thing he could think of to do. He'd have to try.

Hail was turning to water. That's the way it usually went. Hail first, then rain. Well, the country could use some rain. Buck recalled with a wry grin how the grass stopped growing if it didn't rain at least once a week. Rain was mighty important to a cattleman, even if it did get him wet and half-frozen. This was the first rain in ten or twelve days. Cattlemen would welcome it.

Now it was pouring, drumming the ground. The creek was rising. Buck was uphill from the creek, about eight feet up. It would have to rise a lot to reach him. Most of these mountain thunderstorms didn't last that long. The rain would stop soon. In the meantime he was dry and safe. No man would be looking for a chance to shoot him as long as the rain came down that hard. He sat on a big rock inside the cave and prepared to wait it out.

But soon the creek turned into a wild, rampaging torrent. It looked to Buck like the Arkansas River. Its banks were climbing. Boulders that weighed two hundred pounds or more were being rolled around like marbles. Thunder cracked. Lightning zig-zagged overhead. A small aspen that had been torn from the ground was swept downstream, bobbing and twisting in the water, traveling fast.

Lightning was something else that made mountain storms dangerous for a man on a horse. Lightning looked for anything that stuck above the ground, and a man on a horse was an easy mark. The only times that Buck had dismounted and led his horse was during an electrical storm. And that reminded him of something else, something that made him jump up fast.

Granite had been known to conduct electricity. A man sitting on granite during an electrical storm could sure get his ass burned. Buck had to be careful what he touched.

He wished the rain would stop. The grass and ground had to be thoroughly soaked by now, and any more rain would just run off into the low places. That's what it was doing, running into the canyon. From all over up there it was pouring into the canyon. The creek was an angry, swirling, roaring mass. Buck couldn't leave the cave if he wanted to now.

"Come on, stop it," he said, looking up at what he could see of the sky. His answer was a boom of thunder and a bolt of lightning.

He did some mental calculating: if it quit soon, the creek would recede, and by night he'd be able to walk out of the canyon. The longer it continued to pour down, the longer it would take the creek to return to its old banks. Right now a fish couldn't live in that water. It would be beaten to death on the rocks.

Another tree went by, this one a spruce at least twenty feet long. It turned end for end where the creek was wide, then smashed against a boulder and shot downstream like an arrow.

The water was climbing.

"Lord, lord," Buck muttered aloud. "Come on now, stop this damned foolishness." The rain came like water poured out of a barrel. It came in sheets so dense Buck could barely see the other side of the canyon. Down it came. The creek was rising.

Cold. Buck shivered, and wished he had his blanket-lined jacket from the pack panniers. There was no such thing as a warm rain in the mountains. It always turned cold when it rained. Even though he was dry, he shivered. Men had turned blue from being rained on. Turned blue and shivered and shook like an aspen in the wind. Buck remembered a cowboy who'd been out in the cold rain so long he'd turned purple, shivered violently, then went out of his mind and raved like a maniac. Buck and another cowboy had tried to save him. They'd wrapped him in everything dry they could find and held him down until eventually he stopped shivering and raving. He was still then. Too still. Next thing Buck knew the man was dead.

Stop shiverin', Buck Innes, he said to himself. At least you're dry.

For the moment, he was dry. The creek was climbing.

Under his breath, Buck hummed, "I'll bet my money on the . . . lord, lord."

Rain, rain and more rain. No letup in sight. The sky, when Buck stuck his head out of the cave and looked up, was dark. There was no break in the clouds. Funny, but it reminded him of a verse his mother used to recite when he was a little tyke: "Rain, rain go away. Come again another day."

"Yeah, go away. Enough, already. Enough is enough."

Like a mad river, water roared down the canyon, tearing and pushing at everything in its way. Water was now lapping at the pile of rocks in front of the mine. "Damn," Buck muttered, "looks like I'm gonna get my feet wet."

He was right. Water creeped around the rocks, and inch by inch, made its way inside. "Feet, hell," Buck muttered, "I might get my annual bath sooner than I need it."

Inch by inch. Surely, the rain would quit soon. Only a few times in his life had Buck seen rain come down this hard this long. Lord, but he'd like to be sitting on the porch of Mrs. Davenport's boarding house, sitting high and dry and watching water pour off the porch roof. A slug of whiskey would feel mighty good right now too. Whiskey would warm his insides and stop his shivering.

No use getting his boots wet. Water was up to his ankles. Buck sat on a rock, pulled his boots off and stood in water in his sock feet. Damn, the water was cold. Where to put the boots to keep them dry? Looking up, Buck saw a small ledge near the ceiling. A dynamite blast had created a shelf in the rock wall. Reaching over his head, he put his boots up there. Water was up to his knees.

He was going to drown.

Chapter Thirteen

Only a few inches of the rock pile was above water. Buck stood on it in his sock feet, out in the rain, and watched the water climb. His hair was plastered to his head, and he was soaked. He was doomed and he knew it. Even if it stopped raining right now, the water would continue to climb for an hour or more. He was no swimmer. He'd never had to swim. Once, years ago, he'd tried to wade across a swift stream and was knocked off his feet by the force of the water. He remembered that his boots had quickly filled with water, which made wading impossible. But that stream wasn't deep enough to drown in. He'd been able to crawl out on his hands and knees. The water here was deep enough to drown a giraffe and so swift it was moving big boulders.

He was smart, taking off his boots. No man could swim wearing boots full of water. What else could he take off? The Colt? Hell, might as well. Its weight would pull him down in the water, and he'd lose it anyway. Buck unbuckled the gunbelt, waded to the far side of the mine and put the gun, holster and belt on the ledge with his boots. He kept his knife. It was in a sheath fastened to the belt that held his pants up, and it didn't weigh much. Then he climbed to the top of the pile of rocks and watched the water come up to his feet.

Wouldn't be long now. But he wasn't going to jump into the water until he had to. He was standing on the highest spot he could reach, and if he stood there long enough maybe a miracle would happen.

Nope. Water was up to his knees and rising fast. Soon it would knock his feet from under him. He might as well jump and get it over with.

Get what over with? His life, that's what.

Well, Buck, he said to himself, you've lived a long time. You've had your hard times and you've had your good times. If you had it all to do over again, you'd . . . aw, no use thinkin' about that. "Doo-dah."

He jumped.

The water was so cold he felt nothing at first, only numbness. Then he felt himself being pulled, pushed and sucked out toward the middle of the canyon where the water was deepest. Holding his breath, he could only hope that his head would break water soon. Like a pine chip, he spun, bobbed and was pulled along with the stream. For a few seconds he saw the sky, and he exhaled with a grunt then inhaled just before he was flipped head over heels. A boulder was in his way, and he hit it with his left shoulder but he was too numb to feel it. He was spinning, twisting, pushed, pulled.

A mountain of water was pushing him down. The pressure was tearing him apart. His lungs were about to burst. He had to have air. Now he was at the bottom of the stream, where the creek

114

used to be, and he was shooting straight down the canyon. His mind was whirling. Dying was not on his mind, only survival. He had to have air, had to have it. Kicking with his feet, paddling with his arms, he tried to fight his way to the top. Couldn't. No longer able to hold his breath, he opened his mouth and sucked water into his lungs. He felt himself losing consciousness.

Another big boulder was in front of him, and he grabbed at it with both hands, fingers curled, trying desperately with the last ounce of strength he had to hang on. And then his head was clear. He coughed, gasped, coughed, gasped. His lungs would never fill with air again. Too much water. He coughed and gasped until finally he was able to look around, look up at the sky. His head stopped spinning. Strength was returning.

But the water was pulling at him, pulling, pounding, tearing. Grimacing in desperation, he clawed for a finger hold on the boulder. His fingers were slipping off. He was going under again.

And he was gone.

Rolling head over heels, his head hit the gravelly bottom, then he was shooting forward again. His face cleared water long enough for him to suck in a mouthful of air before he was forced on, rolling, twisting. Something solid was pushing at him. Hands flailing, he grabbed at it. He got hold of something that was moving and hung on. When his head broke water again he saw that he had hold of a tree. Never mind what kind of tree. It was floating, with most of its trunk and limbs out of the water.

Buck locked both arms around a limb. He gasped, coughed, gasped and hung on.

115

The tree rolled. The limb Buck was hanging onto went under. He let go with one hand and grabbed for a new hold with the other. The tree kept rolling. He kept grabbing for new holds. It smashed into a boulder and traded ends. Buck held on. Most of the time he was under water, but there were times when he could suck in air. The tree was his lifeline, and he knew it. Scrambling, he got one leg across the trunk. Scrambling some more he got astraddle of it, above water, riding it like a bronc. It pitched, it turned, it rolled. Buck was under water again. Still he hung on. The tree trunk continued rolling, and Buck rolled with it, under water, then above water.

Buck didn't know where in the canyon he was. He was aware of nothing except the necessity of staying with the tree. Constantly grabbing for new holds, trying to keep his head clear, he stayed with it.

It seemed like hours. Would he never get out of the canyon to where the water was shallow? How long could a man wrestle a tree? Buck was losing strength fast. His arms felt like lead. His fingers were turning numb. His face went under and he got a mouthful of water. Coughing, gasping, he felt himself losing consciousness again, his mind going blank.

The tree crashed into something solid and stopped. Water swirled around it, pulled at it, pulled at Buck. His mind flickered to life and ordered him to hang on. It repeated the order over and over: Don't let go. Pull yourself up. He tried. He couldn't do it. He had to do it. Straining every muscle in his body, Buck pulled himself up and got a leg across the tree trunk.

For long moments he stayed there, sputtering and gasping for air. Eventually, he felt strong enough to look around. The tree was lodged sideways between two banks of the stream. The stream narrowed here. It was strong, still pulling, but the tree looked to be stuck solid.

He couldn't believe it. He was alive. Feeling like a drowned rat, but alive. Now, if he had strength enough he could make his way to the bank. Gasping, he waited for strength to return. Felt the tree move. Oh Lord, was it going to tear loose? He had to get to land and do it now.

All right, his mind told him, work your way down the trunk a handhold at a time. Slow, careful. Move your left hand, get a new hold with it. Now the right hand. Keep going, you're gettin' there. Left hand again. Don't let go. Right hand.

His legs were being pulled under the tree. Hanging on was getting more and more difficult. Face screwed up, teeth bared with strain, gray hair hanging in his face, he kept reaching for new handholds nearer the land. Not much farther. Keep goin'. Keep goin'.

There. His feet touched bottom. He could feel it with his toes. Keep going. Now his feet were on something solid. He could move his legs. The bank was almost within reach. Then he stepped on something slick and his feet went out from under him and he felt himself being pulled under the tree. Arms reaching, hands grabbing he got hold of a limb on the other side, pulled himself up. The force of the water was stretching his legs out horizontally. But he could breathe, and he drew air into his lungs in shuddering gasps. He had to reach for another limb, one closer to the bank.

117

Had to hang on for life with one hand and reach with the other. There. He was closer.

The pull of the water wasn't so strong here. He could feel the bottom again. Step carefully and hang onto the tree.

It was mid-afternoon when Buck Innes collapsed on the grass, half in the water and half out of it. He was face down, and he managed to turn over onto his back, but he could move no more.

He wasn't aware that the clouds overhead were swirling and the rain had stopped. He wasn't aware that patches of blue sky could be seen. He was barely aware that he was alive.

After a half-hour he was conscious enough to pull his hips and legs out of the water. And then he started shivering. His clothes, his body, his hair were all sopping wet. He felt like a dishrag that hadn't been wrung out. Lying on his side with his knees drawn up, he shivered. He hugged his knees and shivered. He wanted to get up, but he didn't have the strength. He wasn't aware that the sun had found a hole in the clouds and was shining. All he knew was his teeth were chattering and his whole body was shaking.

It was another hour before Buck felt the warmth of the sun. He realized that he had dozed, and it was a fly buzzing around his face that had awakened him. Sitting up on the grassy bank, he turned his seamed brown face to the sun and enjoyed its warmth. For another hour he sat there. Finally he summoned enough energy to stand. Good old mother earth. It was damp, but boy did it feel good. He stamped his feet to be sure his legs worked.

What had become of his boots? Oh, yeah, back there on a ledge in that mine. So was his Colt Peacemaker. He wondered if the water rose that high. He wondered if he could go back and get them. Nope, not now. The creek was still a wild angry beast. And he was on the west side. Why in hell couldn't he have come out on the east side, the side nearest town. Now he'd have to cross the damned creek again. Aw well, he had to be on the west side anyway to get back to where he'd left his horses. And the girl.

All right, Buck Innes, he said to himself, you're alive. You don't deserve to be, you have no right to be, but by some miracle you're alive.

So, you damned old buzzard, what're you gonna do now?

When he thought of it, that was an easy question to answer: walk. Put one foot in front of the other and walk. In his socks? Well, hell yes, if he had to. And he damned sure had to. He walked. Dammit. If the Almighty had meant for men to walk he would have given them hard hooves instead of tender feet. Too bad he couldn't walk on his hands. His hands were tougher than his feet. Stop bellyachin' you damned old bull, and keep walkin'.

Wait a minute. What if those gunslingers came looking for him? He'd be in a hell of a fix again. No gun, no boots, couldn't shoot, couldn't run. Hell, he didn't even have a hat. Squinting, he studied the country around him. Which side of the creek did those gents end up on? Nothing alive was in sight. Still, he'd better hide and wait until dark.

119

Walking, limping sorely, he went on until he came to a grassy draw. It was the same draw that had saved his life, kept him out of those rifle sights. Here was as good a place to hide as he'd find outside of Shotgun Canyon. Nothing to do but pick a spot where the banks were the steepest and the grass was the tallest, then lie down and rest.

That's what Buck Innes did. The grass was soft, and he was as tired as he'd ever been in his life. He lay on his back with an arm over his eyes to keep the sun out, and within minutes he'd dozed off again.

When he awakened, his stomach was growling from hunger, his hip ached, and the sun was about to go down behind the Continental Divide. Feeling like he was a hundred and fifty years old, he stood. He could have sworn he heard his knees squeak like a rusty gate hinge. Nothing alive was in sight. Well, if they'd looked for him they hadn't found him, and it would soon be too dark to look. Soon it would no longer be necessary to hide. Buck waited until the sun had gone down, then stiff and sore, he climbed out of the draw and started walking.

He walked toward the camp where he'd spent the night before. He didn't know what he'd do when he got there. He'd have to play Indian again and hope for more luck, more than one man was entitled to.

That's all he could do.

Chapter Fourteen

While he hobbled along, sore-footed, Buck realized he had no choice but to go back to his camp.
He had to do what he could for Spooky's daughter if she was still alive, and he had to have
horses. At least one horse. Without a horse he
was as good as dead anyway, and he might as well
die trying. A half-moon put out enough light that
he could see the creek—not only see it but still
hear it. He hoped he'd be able to see the camp
before anyone there saw him. If they were there
the gunsels ought to have a fire—if they could
find something dry to burn. They had to be wet
and cold too. Limping, grunting under his breath,
Buck went on.

It took nearly two hours to limp close to the
place where he and the girl had camped the night
before. He knew he was near there when he saw
the dark shadows of scrub oak, the brush that
had saved his life. He saw no horses. Walking
slow was easy. With his tender feet he couldn't
have hurried if he'd wanted to. Had to be quiet,
though. Watch every step. Keep low. If those gun-

sels saw him he'd head for the brush again. It would probably be useless. Without a gun he couldn't keep them off, and they'd find him eventually. But he'd survived a hell of a lot in the past ten or twelve hours and Old Lady Luck was with him.

Now he was within fifty feet of the spot. The three men should be there. Probably in his bed. His and the girl's. Probably ate their chuck too.

He could see nothing. Ought to see their shapes on the ground. If they were smart they'd keep one man awake and on guard. Ought to see him. Ought to see the horses in the moonlight.

Keeping low, straining his eyes to see in the dark, Buck crept closer. He winced when his left foot came down on a small rock. Either they had no guard or the guard was asleep. Now Buck was at the spot. His groping hands found some empty cans. No ashes from a camp fire. No sleeping men. No beds.

They'd moved. How in hell was he going to find them in the dark? And if he didn't find them in the dark, it would be suicide to find them at all.

A long sigh came out of Buck Innes as he sat on the ground and tried to figure out what to do. Where could they be? Where would he be if he were in their place? Right here. Right here was as good a spot as any. Unless they thought he was armed and looking for them in the dark. They wouldn't know he'd left his gun behind. In the dark they could be as much afraid of him as he was of them. Yeah, that explained it. They were afraid he'd sneak up on them in the dark, and they'd moved. But where? Not toward the end of the canyon. He'd come from that direction. But not too far away from the canyon either. If they were going to claim Spooky's mine they'd have to tear down his claim markers and put up some of their own. Then they'd head for town and the county recorder. Had they done that already? They could have. They could have been lucky enough to do that and get across the creek before the flood.

But what if they hadn't? If they were still on this side of the creek, they weren't far away. All Buck could do was walk around in the dark and hope to find them. Horses should be easy to see in the moonlight. Find the horses, then find the men. Find them, Buck, he told himself, and do it before daylight. He stood and walked, limped and hobbled, staying on a course parallel with the canyon. Feet already sore and getting worse by the minute, he realized, after another hour, that he had little chance of locating them in the dark. He'd have to wait for daylight. If he could spot them at first light and keep out of their sight he might get lucky. Maybe he could catch one of them away from the others with his pants down, Indian his way up behind him and grab his gun.

It was too much to hope for, but it was something.

Buck stayed back near the rim of Shotgun Canyon, under a stunted, twisted spruce and waited for daylight. It occurred to him that he ought to go back and wait under the buckbrush. But as sore as his feet were he didn't want to go back there. At the first sign of light if no one was in sight he'd hobble around and see what he could see. Not too much timber up here. The three men shouldn't be hard to find. Three men and a woman. Hopefully. He sat on the ground and leaned back against the tree. He missed his hat. Why, he asked himself, did he miss his hat? Hell, he didn't know. He was just used to having a hat. Soon his head slumped forward and his chin was on his chest. He slept.

It was the cold that woke him up. In his shirt sleeves, just sitting there, the chilly night air got to him. He shivered, stood, stretched, saw a little light in the eastern sky and figured it was time to rouse around anyway. One step in his sock feet was all it took to get a loud grunt out of him. This couldn't go on. No man could go barefoot in the Rocky Mountains. Not even an Indian could do that. Hell, not even a horse. But go on he must.

Grunting with every step, Buck walked, eyes straining, trying to see ahead of him, behind him and to the west of him. Shotgun Canyon was to the east. With every painful step the sky became lighter, until finally he was able to see as far as the next range of hills. Nothing human or animal was in sight.

Where in hell were they? Did they really cross the creek before the flood? It didn't seem likely, but maybe they did. They sure as hell weren't anywhere around here.

So what now, Buck Innes, he asked himself. He

124

couldn't just stand here. Go back to the mouth of the canyon and see what the creek was doing. Keep his eyes wide open and constantly looking in all directions, and if he saw anyone hit the ground. Make himself as small as possible. He turned and started back.

He couldn't make it. His feet were two huge blisters. This was hopeless. Sitting on the ground, he used his belt knife to cut the bottom half off his shirt. He tore two narrow strips of cloth off his shirt tail and cut the rest in half. Now he had thin cloth tied around each foot. Maybe that would help. He stood and took two tentative steps. Better. Not good, but better. He still had the top half of his shirt to cover his shoulders.

Hobbling on, he made his way back to the spot where he and Spooky's daughter had spent the night. Only a few empty cans remained. What about the markers he'd put up? He limped to the first one, and was surprised to find it the way he'd left it. In fact, Miss Hallows' note was still buried in it.

Now what in hell . . . ? Why didn't they put up their own claim marker? The second pile of rocks was the same. This site was being claimed by Anita Hallows and, so far, nobody else.

Speaking aloud, Buck said, "Now wouldn't that frost your ass?"

What was the shooting all about? Why did they try to kill him? They wanted Spooky's mine, that was the only explanation. Nothing else made sense. They'd followed him and Spooky's daughter from Cripple Creek and when they found the mine

125

they tried to kill him.

"Aw for . . . well, by God . . . huh?" Turning it over in his mind, he grunted, "Huh," again. Nothing made sense.

And where was Spooky's daughter? Did they kill her and hide the body? Were they still around, maybe on the other side of the creek waiting for the water to go down so they could come back over here? Yeah, that was another possibility.

Then something else caught Buck's attention. Horse tracks. He followed them far enough to see that there were five or six. Couldn't be sure how many. But more than three. And they were going east. The whole outfit had left late yesterday sometime after the rain had stopped. They were leading Buck's two horses and the horse that Miss Hallows had ridden. They were headed back to Cripple Creek sure as anything.

"That do beat all." Well, there was only one thing to do, go back to Cripple Creek himself. Would he recognize any of the three gunsels? He tried to recall their faces. There was one who had stood across the creek from him at Spooky's mine. He was a sort of round-faced gent with a thin moustache. He wore his hat tilted on one side of his head like a city slicker. The others he'd never gotten a good look at. He'd been too busy running and hiding. If he happened onto them in town he might not recognize them. But they'd recognize him, and maybe the surprise on their faces would give them away. Maybe. Anyhow, he had to get back. Without a horse.

A long groan came out of Buck. It was two

days on a horse and at least three days for a man on foot. How long for a barefoot man? Hell, forever. Buck started walking.

It occurred to him that his heavy denim pants legs would make better moccasins. He didn't like the idea of having his bare legs scratched by the grass and weeds, but that was better than having his feet so sore he couldn't stand on them. Using his belt knife, he cut his pants off at the knees and wrapped each foot. Yeah, that helped. He walked, limped, hobbled.

Something good had happened. During the night the creek had gone down. It wasn't back inside its normal banks, but it could be waded. These mountain flash floods came and went. And when he got to the creek he saw how the men on horseback had gotten across. The tracks went downstream instead of crossing near the canyon. Buck remembered a broad, grassy meadow about three miles downstream. Flood water would have spread out there and not been so deep and swift. Horses could have waded across the meadow there. Yep, the gunsels were on their way to Cripple Creek.

Buck waded water up to his knees, and the cold water felt good on his sore feet. Then he went upstream, hoping, while he made his way painfully, that the water hadn't risen high enough to reach his boots and gun on a ledge in Spooky's mine. Twice he had to cross the creek to find a place to walk. Once, where the canyon walls rose straight up out of the creek, he had to walk upstream in the water. It was slow going. The creek still had enough force to knock his feet from under him if he wasn't careful.

The sun was overhead, shining down in the canyon, when Buck got to the mine. With a sigh of relief he saw his boots sitting up there on the ledge. The pocket in the canyon wall was littered with debris—rocks, tree limbs and gravel—that had been carried into it by the flood. The claim markers had been washed away, of course. That didn't matter. What mattered was that his boots and six-guns were high and dry. Standing on tiptoe, he took them down, sat on a rock and tried to put the boots on. Couldn't. His feet were swollen.

Aw for . . .

Cold water was supposed to be good for any kind of swelling, and he sure had plenty of cold water. Hobbling to the creek, he sat on another rock, took all the wrappings off his feet and let the water swirl around them. He laid his socks on a smooth granite boulder for the sun to dry. After a half-hour he gathered everything, buckled on his Colt .45 and made his way barefoot back downstream, wading the creek in places, carrying his boots and socks.

In an hour he was out of the canyon, on the east side of the creek and ready to begin his long walk to town. First he let his feet dangle in the creek awhile, then let the sun dry them, then put on his socks. Now came the important test. Carefully, he pulled on his boots. They were tight, but he got them on. Standing, he took a few steps. His feet were still sore, but he could walk.

All right, Buck Innes, he said to himself, it's a

long walk and you'll get hungry, but there's enough mountain streams between here and town that you won't die of thirst. Hell, Spooky Hallows had walked and led his jackasses. Most of these old sourdoughs walked. You'll make it. Get started.

"Doo-dah, doo-dah."

Chapter Fifteen

He walked the rest of the day, walked, rested, walked. His stomach voiced its complaint about the lack of food and he told it to "Shut up." He picked up horse tracks and knew he was following the three gunsels, and knew they were getting farther ahead all the time. A blister formed on his left heel. He climbed a high rocky ridge and half-walked, half-slid down the other side. The grass was slippery enough that he could slide on the seat of his pants as long as he could avoid the rocks. When the blister on his heel broke, he pulled off his boot and wrapped a piece of his pants leg around the heel. Sundown came surprisingly quick. Looking back he realized he hadn't traveled very far. Before dark he picked out a tall spruce on the south side of a hill where he hoped the night breeze wouldn't reach him, tossed rocks and sticks from under the tree and lay down. At first he lay on his back and looked up at the tree tops and the stars, then he lay on his side, then on his back again. There was no way to get comfortable. His stomach growled.

"Shut up."

In the morning, when he started out, his feet were so sore he didn't see how he could continue walking. But walk he did. Part way up another hill he dropped to his knees, then fell over onto the seat of his pants. It took fifteen minutes to gather enough strength to get up. He had to stop and rest three times before he got to the top. Over the top and at the bottom of the other side he came to a small stream. There, he sat on the ground for a half-hour with his bare feet in the water. The pleasant cooling gave him the energy to go on.

But at the end of the day he thought he'd walked as far as he could. His legs were so weak he was stumbling. Sheer exhaustion brought sleep under another tree. Fitful sleep, but sleep just the same. At daylight he forced himself up and on, staggering at times. At noon on that day—the third day—he had little hope of survival. If he didn't see town soon, he'd pass out and never wake up. When he'd started the journey he figured he could make it in three days. He hadn't figured on sore feet.

He came to another small stream that wound through a patch of willows, and stopped again, pulled his boots off and soaked his feet. Back in the willows, he couldn't see the country around him and no one could see him. That was all right. He didn't expect to see anyone anyway. Just let the cool water run over his feet, lie back and rest. Rest here and die here. Funny, his stomach wasn't growling any more. He remembered someone saying once that the first two days without food were the worst. After that a starving man didn't feel anything, just got gradually weaker. A small black water snake went past his head where he lay, and he barely had the strength to watch it wriggle into the water. He didn't have the strength to move. Not ever again. If he had to die, here was a good place to do it.

Horses.

Did he hear a horse? Raising his head, he tried to peer between the willows. Naw, couldn't be. There it was again, the fluttering sound a horse makes when it clears its nostrils. And voices. Men's voices. Now he could hear horses pushing, crashing through the willows. Help was coming. He was going to ride the rest of the way to town.

Wait a minute. Maybe it was the would-be killers headed back to the mine. If it was, he'd better hide. But if it wasn't he sure wanted to attract their attention. They were coming closer. Hide until he could see them. Had to find a place to hide.

Hastily, he pulled on his socks and boots and scrambled up. He tiptoed farther back into the willows and lay on his belly. They were coming, and then they were at the creek. Two men and three horses. They stopped to let the horses drink.

Suddenly, Buck Innes stood and grinned. Doing his best to walk normally, he grinned from ear to ear.

"Say, John," he said, trying to sound casual, "what're you doin' here? You lost?"

132

The two men were sitting their saddles, rein hands low on the horses' necks while the horses had their heads down to drink. One was Deputy Sheriff John Burghart. The other was a man Buck had seen around town, but wasn't acquainted with. Both men jerked their heads around at the sound of Buck's voice, stared a moment, then grinned too. "Buck, you old rounder, what the hell're you doin'? Takin' a walk for your health?" The deputy, a short, round man with a walrus mustache, was sitting on one horse and holding the lead rope of a pack horse that was carrying two bedrolls and two panniers.

"Yeah." He forced strength into his voice. "It's good for the disposition, they say, a sure cure for constipation and everything else that ails you." He stood there, trying to keep his dignity by standing tall and straight. His shirt tail had been cut off above the waist and his pants legs had been cut off at the knees. Hairy legs showed between his knees and the tops of his boots.

"Well, if that's true you oughta be shittin' like a goose 'cause you look like you've walked a long ways. Matter of fact, you look like you tangled with a buzz saw. Where'n hell did you come from anyways?"

"Shotgun Canyon. Know where that is?"

"Not exactly, but we was headin' in that direction. That's where that young woman said she saw you last."

"You wouldn't be talkin' about Miss Anita Hallows, would you?"

"That's her. We thought we'd go see if we could

find your carcass. You're s'posed to be dead. This here is Bert Anderson. He volunteered to come along."

"How do," Buck said, nodding at Anderson, a thin man with a gray beard and a dirty gray hat. "Howdy," said Anderson.

"Dead, I ain't, but I'm sure tired of walkin'. How far to Cripple Creek?"

"Only about four hours. She said you was drowned, and she brought your horses back to Hinson's barn."

"Is she hurt? Anybody with her?"

"Looked tired but healthy, and I didn't see nobody else. Bert, did you see anybody with her?"

"Nope. Seen 'er ridin' down the street a-leadin' two horses, one carryin' a ridin' saddle and the other carryin' a pack saddle."

Buck had to absorb that. It couldn't be. She didn't know how to put a pack saddle on a horse. Hell, she couldn't even saddle her own horse and do it right. She'd gone back to town with the three would-be killers. Running his hand over the top of his bare head, Buck muttered, "That do beat all."

"Huh?" asked Deputy Burghart.

"Aw, nothin'. How about her dad, Spooky Hallows, seen anything of him?"

"No. She said you and her went out there to look for him. I ain't seen or heard nothin' of him for a long time. Any idea what become of him?"

"Naw. Didn't see him at all."

"Well, unless you figure you ain't had enough exercise, climb up on this pack horse. Let's head back to town, and you can tell me what happened out there."

He had to have a leg up, getting on the pack horse. First the load had to be rearranged so the two beds were draped across the pack saddle, then Buck put his left knee in the deputy's hands and got a push up on top of the beds. It was strange, sitting up there, and when the horse moved, Buck had to grab hold of the lash rope to keep from falling off. But anything would have been better than walking.

On the way, he told the deputy no more than he had to. Yeah, he admitted, he did get caught in a flashflood in a canyon. He was in there looking for Spooky Hallows's mine. And, yeah, he damned near did drown. When he found out he was still alive, he couldn't believe it.

"Did you find the mine?"

Instead of answering, Buck went on with his story: the girl had stayed on the canyon rim while he did that, and when she saw the way rain water poured out of the canyon and when he didn't come back, she had a good reason to believe he'd drowned.

"Saw some dark clouds over west a few days ago. Didn't rain a drop here."

"Rain is spotty in this country."

Bert Anderson had been listening quietly. Now he asked again, "Did you say you found old Spooky's mine?"

"No, I didn't say that."

"Oh."

"I reckon Miss Hallows is gonna be surprised

to see me alive."

"She's gonna think she's seein' a ghost. But she'll be happy. She was some sad little woman when she told me about you drownin'. So choked up she almost couldn't talk."

"Sure would like to know what became of her pappy."

They delivered Buck to the porch of Mrs. Davenport's boarding house. Word of his death had reached the landlady and Hadigan, and they were so surprised they looked at each other as if to ask whether they were seeing something that wasn't there. Then Hadigan grinned and allowed he knew Buck was too full of hot air to drown. Mrs. Davenport said her prayers had been answered. The two of them helped Buck to his room. When Mrs. Davenport saw the condition of his feet, she was all sympathy.

"Poor Mr. Innes. You went through all that for a friend. I'll get some warm water for your feet. You don't have to come to the kitchen to eat, I'll bring you something." She left and went to her kitchen.

"Buck," Hadigan said, "where in hell you been, anyways?"

"Aw, nowhere." He added. "Uh, your rifle, I think it's over to Hinson's. I was told my stuff is over there."

"Wal, if it ain't, you got enough spondulics to pay me for it and if you ain't you can owe me."

Buck ate, slept, limped out to the toilet, ate some more and slept. Mrs. Davenport found a pair of her late husband's doeskin slippers for him to wear. He wondered if Anita Hallows had heard he was alive and back in town, and if she had, was she coming to see him. He wondered too if the three gunsels had heard he was back, and if they would try to finish the job. He slept with the Colt .45 within easy reach of his bed.

Next day he was still too sore-footed to walk any father than to the toilet and back, carrying the .45 in his hand. Mrs. Davenport frowned when she saw the gun, but said nothing. Hadigan, though, had to ask, " 'Spect to do some shootin'?"

Buck didn't answer.

It was when he came out of the toilet that luck was with him again. One of the late Mr. Davenport's soft slippers had slipped half-off his foot, and he bent over to pull it back on. A bullet slammed into the wooden door behind him. Instead of straightening up, Buck dropped flat, thumbed the hammer back on the Colt and tried to see where the shot had come from. The most likely spot was over there behind a mine dump, over north. Squinting, gun ready, Buck watched, waited. Nothing moved. Nothing human was in sight. Whoever had fired the shot had backed away from the other side of the pile of low grade ore and disappeared.

Buck waited, staying down, until Hadigan yelled, "Hey, who's shootin'?" He stood in the kitchen door. "Somebody shootin' at you, Buck?"

Without answering, Buck stood. Keeping his eyes on the mine dump, he limped back to the house, still carrying the .45 with the hammer back. At the kitchen door, he let the hammer down, and said to Hadigan, "Does that answer your question?"

"Huh?"

"About why I'm packin' this iron."

"Yeah. Goddamn, Buck, what's goin' on?"

"Aw nothin'."

"Wal, I'm glad Mrs. Davenport's gone to the store."

"Me too," Buck said, grinning a weak grin. "If she was here she'd be on her knees prayin'."

"Goddamn, Buck."

He wanted to talk to Anita Hallows. Rather, he wanted to hear her talk. It would be interesting. Now that he was feeling stronger, Buck's curiosity was about to burst out of his head. How come she was still alive? How come the three gunhands brought her back to Cripple Creek? How come they didn't tear down her claim markers and put up their own? Has anybody filed a claim with the government on the mine in Shotgun Canyon?

And how come some jasper took a shot at him here in town? Does she know anything about that? It had to have been one of those three, afraid he'd recognize them. How come they hadn't tried again? Had they cleared out?

He thought about sending Hadigan to fetch her, but Hadigan would be full of questions too and he might find a way to listen to their conversation. Nope, he had to go to her. One more day and he'd do that.

Wearing the doeskin slippers, Buck chopped his

share of firewood, made his way to the toilet when he needed to and stayed flat on his back on his bed the rest of the time. When he went outside he kept his eyes on the mine dump and the Colt in his hand. After breakfast on the second day he managed to get his boots on. His feet were still sore, but not nearly as bad as they were when he was walking for his life. Before he left the house, he buckled the Colt Peacemaker on and let it, in its holster, hang low on his hip. He was no gunfighter, but he had practiced the fast draw a few times when he was a kid, just for the fun of it. After a few practice draws in his bedroom, he realized he wasn't as quick as he used to be.

Don't go gettin' into any fast-draw shootin' matches, he told himself.

He also told himself that if he happened onto any of the three who'd tried to kill him—and recognized them—he wasn't going to wait for an invitation.

He was going to draw and shoot.

Chapter Sixteen

It was four blocks to the two-story Palace Hotel, but it seemed like four miles. Buck limped along, eyeing every man he saw in the street. Cripple Creek was alive, its pulse racing. Men were getting rich. Excitement was on many of the faces Buck saw. Only the working stiffs, the hard rock miners, looked weary. The plank walks were crowded with pedestrians, and Buck often found himself on a collision course. Sometimes they stepped aside and sometimes he did. There were more saloons than anything else on Bennett Avenue. The hotels, the hardware stores, the grocery mercantiles, were all sandwiched between the saloons. Traffic on the street was heavy with ore and freight wagons, buggies and horseback riders. A railroad engine puffed its way into the station, coming from Florence, clanging its bell. A mine whistle screamed. Buck's first stop was a clothing store where he bought a new silver belly

Stetson. The hat wouldn't look and feel right until he soused it in water and let it dry on his head. That wasn't the best way to break in a new hat—the best way was to work up a sweat while wearing it—but he wasn't planning on working up a sweat in the near future. A brand new hat was better than no hat at all.

Inside the hotel lobby, Buck stepped up to the registration desk, picked up a small bell and shook it. It tinkled. He waited a moment and tinkled it again. Nobody came. The lobby was empty of people. A cash register sat on one end of the desk and a foot-square registration book was on the other end. The wall behind the desk was covered with pigeon holes, a hole for each room. Buck shook the bell a third time. Nobody answered.

Aw hell. Damned if he was going to stand there all day tinkling that bell, and he sure didn't walk over here on sore feet for nothing. He turned the registration book around so he could read it and scanned the first two pages. Anita Hallows's name wasn't on them. Flipping back a page, he scanned two more pages and saw her name: Anita Hallows. Denver, Colo. Room one-oh-eight.

All right, he'd just go upstairs and knock on the door of room one-oh-eight.

Wooden stairs creaked as he climbed them and floorboards creaked as he limped down the hall, looking for her room. The doors were all numbered and her room was easy to find. Now.

Won't she be surprised. What will she do?

Faint? He had it planned, he'd just stand there and grin at her until she did something. Maybe she'd slam the door in his face. If she did, he'd knock on it until she opened it again. This was going to be fun.

He knocked. Lightly at first, then louder. He heard bedsprings squeak and footsteps coming to the door. The door opened.

"Oh, uh, excuse me, mister." Buck was flustered and embarrassed. The man who stood before him was barefoot and his shirt tail was out. He looked to be a salesman of some kind. "I, uh, I was lookin' for somebody else."

The door slammed shut.

For a moment Buck stood in the hall trying to figure out what went wrong. He squinted at the room number again, wondering if he'd misread it. Nope. Finally, he shifted his new hat to a more comfortable position and went back down the hall and back down the stairs. The lobby was still empty. He turned the registration book around and found Miss Hallows's name again. Room one-oh-eight. No mistake about that. In one-oh-six was a Dudley White and in one-ten was a woman named Johnson. Flipping back to the first two pages, he ran his fingers down the list until he saw room one-oh-eight. A William Quilhorst had signed for that room. Let's see, oh, he registered August twenty-three. That would be, uh, yesterday. Anita Hallows was no longer there.

"Sir, do you wish to register?" The questioner was a little man with a billy goat beard, a wide

142

necktie, a stiff white collar and a finger-length striped coat. "Are you looking for a room?"

"Oh, no," Buck said. "I was lookin' for Miss Anita Hallows. Is she still here?" He knew she wasn't but he had to ask.

"No sir. She checked out several days ago."

"Do you know where she went?"

"I believe she mentioned that she was going back to Denver."

"She did, huh? Uh, thanks."

"You're the second gentleman to come here looking for Miss Hallows."

"Huh?" That caught Buck by surprise. "I am? Who else?"

The billy goat beard bobbed as the little man chewed on his cheek, forehead wrinkled in thought. "As I recall—it was, oh, a week ago, I believe—he gave his name as Shoeman, or Shoefellow. No, it was Shoemaker."

"Shoemaker? What did he look like?

"Oh, he was younger than you, looked like a working man."

"Was he a little man, about five eight, and kinda thin?"

"No, he was taller than that and husky."

"Did he say what he wanted her for?"

"No. I didn't ask. It was while she was gone. I didn't know it at the time—she made arrangements with the night manager—but she had left her suitcase here in our storage room, saying she would be back."

"Did this Mr. Shoemaker ever come back?"

"Not that I know of. She came back and

stayed one night and left the next day."

"He was a workin' man, you say? A prospector, maybe?"

"I, uh, don't know. He was wearing overalls, the kind with a bib and suspenders."

"Well . . ." Buck could think of nothing more to say, so he said simply, "Thanks."

Outside on the wooden planks Buck ran it through his mind. Somebody had come here looking for her. It wasn't Spooky. Spooky was below average in height, hungry-looking and tough as a boiled owl. Besides, if Spooky showed up in Cripple Creek he wouldn't be here ten minutes until somebody recognized him. Whoever was looking for her didn't find her. Now she'd gone back to Denver. Or so she told the hotel clerk. Where else would she go? And why go anywhere?

Suddenly, he turned on the planks and limped as fast as he could down the street to the county recorder's office.

It was another two blocks to the one-room log building, and by the time he got there he was wishing he was back in the boarding house, wearing the doeskin slippers and sitting on the porch. Inside, he stepped up to a waist-high wooden counter and waited for the woman behind it to quit riffling papers in a desk drawer, turn around and acknowledge that he was there. She was middle-aged with gray-streaked brown hair pulled straight back and tied in a knot behind her head. The knot interested Buck. It looked like the rosebud he used to tie in the end of catch ropes, and he wondered if she tied it with three strands or four. Finally, she closed the drawer. "Yes?"

How did he ask? Buck stammered, "I'm . . . I found some color about a hundred miles west of here, west and south, and I wonder if anybody has claimed that territory."

"Well, did anyone leave claim markers there?"

"Well, yeah."

"Is there a name on the markers?"

"Anita Hallows, I believe."

"Exactly where are these markers?"

"Well, they're in a canyon that us ranchers call Shotgun Canyon."

"Yes."

"Yes?"

"Yes, a Miss Anita Hallows did file a mining claim on twenty acres in a location she described as Shotgun Canyon, an estimated one hundred and twenty miles west by southwest."

"She did?"

"Yes. Isn't that what you wanted to know?"

"Yes." That was all he could say, except, "Much obliged."

It didn't make sense. No sense a-tall. Not one damned little bit. She came to Cripple Creek to find her father. She didn't find her father but she found his mine. Three men tried to kill Buck, but they didn't hurt her. Instead they brought her back to Cripple Creek. She filed a claim on the mine and then got out of town.

She'd be back. For some reason she'd had to go to Denver, but a mining claim in El Paso

County wouldn't do her any good there. She'd want to sell her claim, and she had to come back to Cripple Creek to do that. Yeah, she'd sell it. In fact, when word got out that gold was found at Shotgun Canyon, other prospectors would be looking for the spot, and when they found it they'd start digging and blasting all over there.

If they could find it.

They would. It might take a while, but they'd find it. And if it was discovered that she owned the best vein, she could sell for a pile of money. Yeah, maybe she was playing it smart. Wait until others proved there was gold in Shotgun Canyon, or on its rim, then write her own check.

What should Buck do about it? Nothing. It wasn't his business. Spooky had to be dead, and if anyone cashed in on his find it ought to be his daughter. So go on back to the boarding house, Buck Innes, forget it and let your feet heal.

He thought he'd never make it back. Each step was more agonizing than the last. Hadigan saw him coming and met him a half-block from the boarding house. He tried to help, but Buck wasn't about to be carried. Finally in his room, Buck sat on his bed and pulled the boots off. Mrs. Davenport brought him a pan of hot water to soak his feet in. He soaked his feet until the water turned cool, then lay back on the bed. His new Stetson hung on a bed post. Naw, it was none of his business what Anita Hallows did.

But he couldn't just forget the whole thing,

and he sure had some questions for her when she came back.

Buck Innes didn't put his boots on again for two days. He lazed around the house, sat on the porch, limped out to the toilet carrying the .45, and stayed off his feet as much as he could. For a while one evening he sat in the kitchen and watched Mrs. Davenport work, watched the way her hips moved inside the long dress, tried to visualize her naked. But her conversation eventually drove him out.

"Some people have no decency at all," she exclaimed.

Buck, thinking she'd caught him staring at her backside, was embarrassed and was trying to find the words for an apology. But she went on: "The very idea, putting stolen gold ore in the collection plate at church."

"Well, uh, ahem, how do you know it was stolen?"

"Why else would a body be carrying it in their pocket? Of course it was stolen. Everybody knows these miners steal from the mines where they work."

"Well, sure, everybody does it when they can get away with it, but it's no crime. The judge ruled that it ain't agin' the law."

"It's a sin. The Good Book says so. Stealing is a sin."

"Yeah, well, the wages these mine muckers have to work for, if they didn't do a little highgradin' now and then they'd have a hard time feedin' their families."

"My husband didn't steal. He was a God-fearing man and he read the Good Book every night."

"Your husband was a mine foreman, not a mucker. He got paid more."

"Just the same he could have stolen if he had been the kind."

"Did, uh, the preacher keep the ore?"

"Well, I don't know, I . . ."

Hah!, Buck felt like saying. He felt like saying, The preacher sold it, didn't he? Now tell me it's a sin. But he didn't. Instead, he stood and said, "Think I'll go set on the porch for a while."

"Supper will be ready in half an hour."

Hadigan was already out there with his boots on the porch rail and his chair tilted back. Buck sat and put his feet in the doeskin slippers on the rail. "What was the Old Lady talkin' about?" Hadigan asked.

"Aw she's pissin' and moanin' about some high-grader leaving a hunk of ore in the church collection plate."

"Might as well give it away," Hadigan said. "Can't sell it no more."

"How come?"

"That assayer that was buyin' it, they run him off a long time ago. Way I heard it they thumped hell out of 'im and gave 'im two days to get his ass out of here or they'd bury 'im here. The mine owners did. They hired a bunch of tough Micks from Denver to beat the shit out

148

of anybody that got caught high-gradin'."

"Reckon they got a right to protect their property."

"Yeah, it was a good thing for a while, but good things don't last long."

"That puts me in mind of somethin'," Buck said. "A feller was here 'while back lookin' for a room. Didn't he move in with you?"

"Naw. Said my room wasn't big enough. I offered to up my ante to Mrs. Davenport, and she said she'd think on it."

"I like the way things are. If I have to pay a couple dollars more I'll do it."

"Me too."

"She's cookin' chicken and dumplin's for supper. Got the chicken from that woman that raises 'em across town."

"The way my guts're talkin' you'd think I ain't et for a week."

"I sure do know that feelin'."

It was the next day that Buck got his boots on and went for a walk. His feet were almost as good as new now. Out of curiosity, he strolled over to the railroad depot and asked Oldham the ticket agent if he'd recognized Miss Anita Hallows when she left.

"Shore, Buck," the agent said, peering from under his green eyeshade. "I seen her before in the hotel restaurant. Her and that dandy came in here together and he watched while she bought a ticket and boarded Number Sixteen."

"She was with somebody?"

"Yup. Gent name of White. Dudley White."

"Well, I'll be damned," Buck said, turning away. Dudley White.

Where had he heard that name before?

Chapter Seventeen

He was on his way to George Hinson's barn when it came to him. Switching directions, he hot-footed it to the Palace Hotel. He wanted another look at that registration book. But he didn't get it. The little man with the billy goat beard was behind the desk, sorting mail and putting it in the pigeon holes.

"Listen," Buck said, "I know I'm a lot of bother and I know you're a busy man, but I was helpin' Miss Anita Hallows look for her dad, and I'm tryin' to find out what become of her."

"Miss Hallows? She hasn't come back. You are looking for her father, you say? Is he the Mr. Hallows who has a very rich mine somewhere?"

"He's the one, but he ain't been seen for a month or so. Now she's gone too."

"Oh, I see, umm."

"Was there a Dudley White here at the same time she was?"

"Hmm." The little man ran a finger around his high tight collar. "I remember a gentleman named

Dudley White. Let's see . . ." He pulled the registration book to his side of the desk and scanned the pages. Turning pages, he finally exclaimed, "Yes, here he is. Hmm."

"Was he here at the same time she was?"

"Hmm, yes. They both were gone for a few days and they came back on the same day. Yes. Hmm. He left the day after she did."

"Excuse me for askin' so many questions. When she came here the first time, did he, uh, was he here?"

The little man's forehead wrinkled in thought. He stroked his beard, then flipped pages, studied them. "No. She arrived on the, uh, August eleven. He arrived on the thirteenth."

"Did you ever see them together?"

"No. I don't remember seeing them together. That is, until they checked out. But I believe that was a coincidence."

It was Buck's turn to say, "Hmm."

"Did you find Mr. Hallows's mine?"

"Can't say I did. What does this Dudley White look like? Has he got a little thin moustache and a kind of round face? About my size, only younger?"

"Why, yes. As I recall, that describes him fairly well."

"Did he wear his hat on one side of his head like a city slicker?"

"Yeah, as I recall, he did."

"Thanks. I'm much obliged."

At the Royal Flush saloon, Sheets, the bartender, allowed, "You look like you ain't all here,

152

Buck. You gonna drink that whiskey or stare it to death?"

"I paid for it and I can stare at it if I want to."

"Yeah. Yeah, you can." Sheets went down the bar to talk to another customer.

He felt like a fool. He was a fool. Damn near got himself killed to help out a girl who didn't care whether he lived or died. The more he thought about it the worse he felt. "How plain damned stupid can a man get?" he said aloud.

"You talkin' to me, Buck?" Sheets asked, insulted.

"Naw," Buck answered without looking up, "I'm talkin' to the biggest damned fool the world has ever seen."

"Yourself?" Sheets chuckled, "It's all right to talk to yourself, but if you're gonna fight with yourself go outside, will you?"

"I oughta. I oughta choke myself, I'm so damned dumb." He tossed the whiskey down his throat, said, "Aaagh," and left.

The word was out now, and they began walking up the path to Mrs. Davenport's boarding house, looking for Buck Innes. Buck asked Mrs. Davenport to tell them he wasn't there, but she refused to lie. "However," she said, "I will tell them you are not feeling well and do not wish to receive visitors."

"Aw, what's the use."

The first few were prospectors in their jackboots and baggy wool pants held up by suspenders. They offered to give Buck a share of any rich ore they found in the place called Shotgun Canyon. All he had to do was tell them how to get there.

"Is that sure 'nuff where old Spooky's mine is?" asked one skinny man with a week's growth of whiskers.

"Somebody's been blastin' there and takin' out some rocks and it had to of been Spooky Hallows."

"Then she's a rich 'un. There's got to be more'n one vein. I'll give you half of what I find."

Shaking his head, Buck said, "I made a promise to Spooky's daughter. I can't break a promise."

"I'll find 'er anyway. You c'ld save me some huntin', that's all."

One of the callers was no prospector. He was plump, soft, and dressed in fine wool clothes with a cravat at his throat and a high beaver hat on his head. "Excuse me, sir, I am trying to locate a Mr. Innes, and I was advised that I might find him at this address."

"I'm Buck."

"Sir, allow me to introduce myself, I am Mr. Jackson Stephens, attorney at law. I represent a group of investors who are interested in the gold mining industry. I, the uh, county recorder, has advised me that a valuable mine first discovered by a Mr. Andrew Hallows has been located in an area called Shotgun Canyon. I've been advised that you have been there and know exactly where it is. May I ask, is that correct, sir?"

Buck took his feet off the porch rail and

crossed his legs. "Yeah, I've been there."

"May I ask, sir, did you find a valuable mine there?"

"I found a mine, but I wouldn't know gold if it stood up and shook hands with me."

"Ha, ha." The lawyer's chuckle held no mirth. "Uh, Mr. Innes, my clients are prepared to offer you a substantial fee if you would guide their engineers to the site."

"I can't do that."

"We will provide all the animals, supplies and equipment that you might need."

"Like I told all them other fellows, I made a promise to the daughter of Spooky, er, Andrew Hallows. I've got a hunch she'll be back in town soon, and maybe you can deal with her."

"I understand she lives in Denver and has returned there, do you know when she will return to Cripple Creek?"

"No. Just a hunch. She'll be back."

"Do you know her address in Denver?"

"No sir, I don't. I really don't."

"You won't reconsider our offer? Your fee would be substantial."

"Not likely."

"Well, if, after giving it some thought, you decide to reconsider, my offices are in the Baker Building over the Baker Mercantile."

"I'll remember that."

"When Miss Hallows returns, would you direct her to my offices?"

"Yeah, I'll do that."

"Thank you very much, Mr. Innes."

155

After he left, Buck went to his room and flopped down on the bed. He wasn't surprised that gold hunters were wearing down the path to his door. It was impossible to keep a valuable find a secret. Gold hunters checked with the county recorder every day to see who had filed a claim where. That's why Spooky never filed a claim. He wanted the whole section to himself. And when the gold hunters saw the name Hallows on a claim, they got excited. What did puzzle Buck, when he thought about it, was why it took them so long to come calling.

Sitting up suddenly, he pulled on his boots and stomped out of the house. He was going to have to ask more questions.

The knot in her hair was no rosebud, Buck decided. It looked more like a Gilligan hitch tied with two strands. Didn't matter. Buck stood back against the wall until two other men left, then he stepped forward.

"Yes?"

"Remember me?"

"Yes."

"Well, I was wonderin' why nobody else came in here and saw that Miss Hallows had filed a minin' claim."

"Until recently, nobody asked."

"But there's always somebody comin' in here to see what was filed. How come you didn't tell 'em about Miss Hallows?"

"Why, I . . ." She was suddenly flustered.

"Did somebody pay you to keep mum?"

"Sir, I do not lie. I did not lie to you when you asked and I did not lie to anyone else."

"Oh, I get it. You just didn't volunteer the information, is that it?"

Face red, her fingers went to the knot at the back of her head, fumbled with it. For a few seconds, Buck thought she was going to untie it. "I have a lot of work to do here. Sometimes it doesn't occur to me to tell everyone who comes in here everything that happens."

"Somebody paid you."

"Sir, I must ask you to leave. If you do not I shall report you to the authorities."

This was getting nowhere. "All right, all right," Buck said, trying to cool his own anger as well as hers. "Tell me this much, who else has filed claims in or on top of Shotgun Canyon?"

"Well, I . . ."

With an exasperated sigh, Buck said, "I don't know nothin' about the law, ma'am, but I don't think you're s'posed to keep that kind of information a secret."

"Very well, you can look for yourself." She opened a desk drawer and took out four sheets of paper. Buck didn't have to read every word. Two words almost jumped off the paper at him: Dudley White. Then there were Anita Hallows, Benjamin Gotswald and James Butcher. Spooky's daughter and three men. The three who'd tried to kill him.

But since he'd got back to Cripple Creek another name had come up. "Uh, ma'am, does a gentleman name of Shoemaker have a claim around there?"

"Shoemaker? I don't recall a Shoemaker."

"Hmm."

"Here is the map that covers that general area." She spread a U.S. Geological Survey map on the counter. To Buck, it was nothing more than a big sheet covered with swirls. The woman said, "It doesn't identify the canyons and streams by name. They haven't been named."

Buck had never seen a map of that kind, and it meant nothing to him. All he could do was shake his head. "I know that country as good as anybody, but I couldn't find my own homesteads on this map."

With a haughty smile, she said, "Only the educated can read a topographical map."

Still shaking his head, all Buck could say was, "Much obliged."

Next, he directed his steps toward Hinson's barn. He was limping again by the time he got there. "Heered you was back and ornery as ever," George Hinson said, pushing his hat back and wiping his forehead with a polka dot bandana. "Wondered when you was comin' over to see to your horse and get your stuff. How's your ass?"

"Never mind my ass. How's my bay horse?"

"He's doin' all right now. Purty ganted up when that girl brung 'im back. So was my horses. She must of forgot to let 'em graze."

"I'm surprised she got 'em back. Brought my bed and stuff back took, huh? How about Hadigan's rifle?"

158

"Yeah, it's all over there in my harness room."

He grabbed a halter off a wooden peg in the wall and walked out into the small pasture. His bay horse was easy to catch. Buck looked him over and picked up his fore feet one at a time, checking the shoes. "You ready to go again, feller? I'll take better care of you than those gunsels did."

Everything he needed was already there in Hinson's barn, everything but groceries. Limping, Buck went to Baker's mercantile and bought enough groceries to last a week, carried them to the boarding house.

"Looks like you're travelin' again," Hadigan said.

"Yep. Up to now I've done everything wrong. I didn't find Spooky, and all I did was lead a bunch of crooks and killers to his mine. I've got to go back and see if I can undo some of the dumb things I did."

Chapter Eighteen

He rode back over the same route he'd walked. There was no trail, but he was following horse and mule tracks. The tracks went both ways, and the ones going west weren't more than a few days old. He reckoned there were two horses and two mules going west. At mid-morning the first day out from Cripple Creek, the tracks veered to the north. Buck drew rein and tried to figure out why. If they were going to Shotgun Canyon they were going in the wrong direction. Maybe they didn't know the way.

Yeah, that was it. Somebody was looking for Shotgun Canyon and wasn't likely to find it. Buck rode on, leading a pack horse carrying his bed, coffee pot, skillet, tin plate, axe and some groceries. He kept Hadigan's 30-30 in a boot under his right knee, and he carried the Colt six-gun on his right hip. There were more horse tracks. These were older and going west by southwest. Four or five horses. Then these tracks turned the wrong way too. Too far south.

A few miles ahead he saw them again. Now

they were going in the right direction. Nope. They were wandering. Somebody had looked for landmarks and hadn't found any. Buck reckoned it was the three would-be killers. The tracks were about the right age and number. "Huh," he grunted aloud, finding town with roads running north and south out of it had been easy. Finding their way back to Shotgun Canyon wouldn't be so easy.

Maybe they wouldn't find their way back. No, they'd find their way. They knew the general direction and they might wander too far north or south at times, but eventually they'd find it.

There were no obvious landmarks to look for. Buck relied on a lifetime of experience in figuring directions by the sun and a lifetime on horseback in the mountains, taking careful notice of everything he saw. The trees, hills, boulders, draws and ridges were not all alike to a practiced eye. But describing them to someone would have been impossible. Buck knew exactly where he was and where he was going.

He crossed mountain ridges covered with boulders and tall timber. He crossed narrow grassy valleys, pushed through willows and forded shallow streams. Riding by a spot where he'd once spent the night, half-dead, he shook his head sadly. He remembered well the feeling of hopelessness, of staggering on and on, of getting weaker by the hour, afraid he was going to die. Lord, how he'd hate to do that again. He reached down and scratched the bay horse's neck and spoke aloud, "The Almighty knew what he was

161

doin' when He made horses."

The sky had been a clear blue in the morning, but was now dark and threatening. Thunder rolled across the sky. Buck had a long yellow slicker tied behind the cantle of his saddle, but he reckoned it would be a waste of time to get down and put it on. He'd never bet that it wouldn't rain and he'd never bet that it would until the rain actually fell. A few fat drops splattered his shoulders and arms. That was all. Ten minutes later the sun was shining over west, and the sky was streaked with different shades of gray and purple.

The pain in his right hip was bringing a grimace to Buck's face, but he continued on until sundown, then camped next to a stream almost hidden in dense willows. Supper was one of two beefsteaks he'd wrapped in wax paper, coffee, fried potatoes and bread. After he ate he took a look at the horses to be sure the hobbles weren't soring their ankles. Then he folded back the tarp and blankets on his bed, pulled off his boots and crawled in. He kept his sixgun under the blankets.

The constant ache forced him to lie on his left side. And while he lay awake, he tried again to think of a plan, something he could do when he got to Spooky's mine. The problem was the mine belonged to Anita Hallows and her friends now. They had a legal claim to it. There was no legal way to get them out of it. Buck would have to do something illegal.

By noon the second day he was miserable. He had to get down and walk. After convincing himself that no other human was in sight, he did something he'd never done before and wouldn't want to be seen doing; he walked and led his horses. For a half-hour he stayed afoot. Then his feet began to hurt. What was worse, sore feet or a throbbing ache in his right hip? He got back on his horse and rode, sitting on his lift hind cheek as much as possible, something else he wouldn't want to be seen doing. A man who sat a saddle that way had never ridden anything but the gentlest of horses. Any other kind would jump from under him. He rode up the hills and walked down them.

An hour before sundown he reckoned he could reach the east rim of Shotgun Canyon by dark or shortly after. Wanting to get there in broad daylight, he made his camp in a thick grove of aspen that bordered a stream. His horses had good grazing in the tall bunch grass that grew among the trees. There were almost as many downed trees as standing ones. Aspens were fragile. They grew fast and died fast. A small black bird that thought its territory was being invaded repeatedly dived at him until he took off his new Stetson and threatened to swat it.

"Aw, go on," he said, not unfriendly. "I ain't here to bother you or your nest, so you just mind your own business and I'll mind mine."

By the time the sun showed itself over the eastern horizon next morning, Buck was saddled and traveling. He figured it was a ninety-minute ride to Shotgun Canyon. The mining claims he'd seen in the county recorder's office took in twenty acres each, and that included both sides of the canyon and a big section of the canyon itself. Boundary markers should be on each side.

All right. Buck remembered a timbered hill about a half-mile from the east rim, east and a little north of Spooky's mine. He turned his horses in that direction. Before he got there he crossed horse tracks again. Four or five horses. They could have been left by the same bunch whose tracks he'd followed the first day out of Cripple Creek. Probably were. Whoever had left them was lost for a couple of days, then found their way. At least these tracks were headed in that direction. There was no way of telling whether the horsemen were Anita Hallows's three cohorts or prospectors looking for Spooky's mine. It was doubtful anyone except Buck and a few old time cattlemen could ride directly to it. Even the three hoodlums who'd been there would probably lose their bearings at least once.

There were men looking, that was for sure. The territory around Spooky's mine could be crowded with prospectors or there could be nobody there. Buck wanted to find out before he showed himself. That's what he had in mind when he rode into the timber, the last cover between him and the canyon rim.

He no more than got into the timber when he realized someone had been there before him. Not lately, though. Old ashes from a campfire were almost covered by this year's grass. That meant they had to have been more than a year old. And burro droppings were decomposed almost to nothing.

Burro droppings meant a prospector had camped here and that meant Spooky Hallows. And that puzzled Buck. Why would Spooky camp here when his mine was way over there? Oh. A possible answer came to Buck. Here, Spooky was in the timber where he wouldn't be so easy to see. Yeah, he was probably on his way back to Cripple Creek, and decided to spend the night here after crossing the creek and getting on his side of the big ditch. This was a little out of the way, but it was cover. Spooky was always looking for cover. That's how he got his nickname.

Sitting his saddle, staring down at the long-dead ashes, Buck wished they could talk, that Spooky's spirit would rise out of them and tell him what had happened. A little divine advice on what to do about it all would have been welcome too. The thought that went through Buck's mind was; I apologize, old friend. I wanted to find you or your mine so your daughter could claim it. I didn't mean to bring a bunch of killers to it. I hope you understand that.

With a sad shake of his head, Buck rode on, then pulled up again—suddenly. He spoke aloud, "Now what in holy hell is this?" What he was staring at was a pile of rocks. Not rocks the way thousands of years of wind, rain, freezing and thawing had left them, but rocks blasted apart by dynamite and a pick and shovel. Shattered rocks left here by a man. By Spooky Hallows. Gold ore? Why else would Spooky have carried them out of the canyon? But why leave them here? It looked as if he'd unloaded the pack boxes on one of his burros right here.

Buck dismounted stiffly, picked up a rock as big as his fist and examined it. It was granite with a light streak running through it. Kicking at rocks to scatter them, he saw a white one, picked it up and examined it. Quartz. He'd heard that prospectors looked for quartz, among other things, and he'd heard that only a man who knew what he was doing would recognize gold. In fact, he remembered Spooky himself once saying, "All that glitters ain't gold, and gold don't glitter nohow."

Buck had seen a pile of rocks like this before, near Spooky's cabin. Why in all that's holy did Spooky leave this pile here? Squatting on his heels, Buck tried to figure it out. Maybe, he thought, one of the burros went lame and couldn't pack the load. Yeah, that could be. Spooky could have unloaded him here and figured on coming back for this stuff, then got himself killed. No, that couldn't be. Spooky was seen in Cripple Creek not much more than a month ago, and these rocks have been here longer than that. Brown pine needles were scattered among them, needles that had blown off the trees last fall and winter. Well, maybe he hadn't been in a hurry to come back for them. There was plenty of ore where these rocks came from, and it was unlikely that anyone would stumble over them. Yeah, he figured on taking his sweet time. That was the only explanation Buck could think of.

But as he mounted and rode on, leading his pack horse, the explanation somehow didn't ring true.

He left his horses in the timber, not far from the gold ore, and walked, carrying the 30-30, to the edge of the forest. There he could look out across a shallow valley to Shotgun Canyon. Squatting again, he studied the country on this side of the canyon and what he could see of the terrain on the west side. He could see where someone had camped near the east rim, had spent the night there before going on next morning to the mouth of the canyon. Sunlight bounced off an empty tin can. Grass had been grazed on and trampled down by horses. The only living creatures he saw were two ravens flapping and cawing above the canyon.

Buck stayed where he was for a good ten minutes, his eyes taking in everything, while he tried to figure out what to do. Finally, he went back to the horses and mounted. He'd go around the south end of the canyon, get into the hills, then cross the creek and get into the grassy draw that had once provided the cover he'd needed to survive gunfire. First, he wanted to see if there were any claim markers on this side.

Eyes busy, seeing every bird, every ground squirrel, every blade of grass that moved in the breeze, he rode forward. The 30-30 was in a boot under his right knee and the Colt Peacemaker sat on his right hip. Every hundred feet or so he reined up, twisted in his saddle and looked back, looked in all directions. Still nothing human in sight. Whoever had come here ahead of him was on the other side now or down in the canyon.

Claim markers were easy to see. At the first one, Buck got down and kicked over rocks until he spotted the piece of paper. He pulled it out, unfolded it and read: James Butcher. A quarter of a mile farther on he found another. That paper read, Benjamin Gotswald. The next one read, Anita Hallows, and the last one Dudley White. Buck figured there should be another, one that read, Shoemaker, but no other was in sight. The four he did find claimed a large piece of land along Shotgun Canyon, and there were no doubt markers on the other side too. The four had the whole territory claimed. Anyone else who came along would have to look for color two or three miles away from Spooky's find.

No matter how many gold hunters came along and no matter how many men they were willing to kill, they couldn't jump these four claims. Everything was filed legally with the county recorder, and as Buck understood the law all the claimants had to do to get a patent on the land was to produce some gold ore, or some other valuable metal. That, no doubt, was what the three killers were doing now, looking for rich ore to take back to Cripple Creek. With that they could not only get a patent, they could sell their claims. And probably for enough money to go back to Denver and live in high style.

Even while such thoughts were going through Buck's mind, he heard a muffled BOOM come from the canyon below him. A cloud of dust blew out of the canyon behind the noise. Yep, they were blasting, looking. Buck hobbled his horses and walked, bending low, to the rim of the canyon. Lying on his stomach, he looked down and saw them. Sure enough, there was the round faced gent with the smart little mustache. The others had to be his two cohorts. They were busy hammering on a double jack, punching a hole in the granite at the end of the mine, making a place to put dynamite. After taking it all in, Buck backed away, went to the horses, mounted and rode on. He was soon in the low hills on the south end. There, he crossed the creek. The stream was narrow now, but it was easy to see that it had recently been a high, raging river. Driftwood was scattered for fifty feet on each side of the stream, and the grass was matted.

Remembering the rampaging river caused Buck to cast a fearful glance at the sky. Only a few white clouds floated overhead. When he got into the draw, he dismounted and led his horses. The draw wasn't deep enough to hide a man on a horse. It wasn't deep enough to hide a standing man, for that matter. But hopefully, the three gunsels were still in the canyon and wouldn't come out for a while. Just the same, Buck didn't want to stick up above the ground any more than he had to. He felt safer, less of a target, on foot. Before he was close to the mouth of the canyon, he crawled on his knees to the edge of the draw and studied the terrain around him. From here he could see the patch of buck brush that had hidded him from killers, and he could see the spot where he and Spooky's daughter had camped. Horses were picketed there. Four of them.

That wasn't surprising. The men were blasting in the canyon, and they had to leave the horses on the rim where there was feed and where they wouldn't be hit by flying rocks. Bedrolls were there too, and camp supplies—a dutch oven, a skillet, a coffee pot. But no men. The men were collecting rich ore. Spooky's ore.

Buck Innes sat on the edge of the draw and tried to figure out his next move. He had no idea what to do.

But, damnit, he had to do something.

Chapter Nineteen

The sun was about an hour and a half from its zenith when Buck reached a decision. There still was nobody at the camp. That would make it easy to do what he had in mind. It was a mean trick, what he had in mind, but after all they'd left him afoot. They'd tried to kill him, almost caused him to drown, then took his horses and left him to walk on sore feet for over a hundred miles. Well, by God, he'd do the same to them.

To do it he had to be horseback, right out in the open country, a good target. He mounted and rode out of the draw, leading the pack horse. With eyes constantly catching every movement, he rode up to the closest of their four horses, dismounted and used his belt knife to cut the picket rope, leaving about eight feet still fastened to the horse's halter. He tied that horse to the crossbucks on his pack saddle. Then he went to the next one, cut the picket rope and tied that one to the tail of the first horse. Knowing that any of the three men could walk out of the canyon, see him and blaze away with a rifle, Buck kept horses between him and the canyon mouth as much as he could. Soon he had three of the horses tied head to tail and the first one tied to his pack horse. Then he mounted and kicked his bay saddle horse with spurless boot heels.

It took a while to get that many horses into a trot, but the bay saddle horse pulled, the pack horse pulled and eventually the whole string of horses was traveling at a trot back down the draw away from the mouth of the canyon. Buck expected to hear a shout and a shot any second, but nothing happened. Still, he didn't breathe easy until he was across the creek and in the hills on the east side of it. He kept the string traveling until he was a quarter mile away from the canyon, headed toward Cripple Creek. Then he untied the four horses, kept a good hold on his two, waved his hat, and hollered. At first the four couldn't believe they were free. When they finally realized it, they took off at a high trot. Two of them broke into a run, kicking up their heels with the pleasure of running free.

Grim-faced, Buck knew that what he'd just done was a serious crime. Leaving a man afoot was as bad as murder. He only hoped that if it came to a trial in court, he'd get a chance to tell the jury what the three men had done to him. He doubted a jury would convict him. And there was a good chance it wouldn't come to a trial. He could be dead or the three gunsels could be dead. And even if they all survived, maybe they'd be afraid to complain to the law. They could be charged with crimes too.

X He watched the free horses until they'd run a mile or more on east. They all wore different brands, and they'd no doubt been bought from a horse trader, probably George Hinson. That didn't mean they'd go back to Hinson's place. No, they'd probably graze along happily until the snow flew and then they'd turn up in some rancher's hay meadow.

Right here, Buck decided, was the place to loosen saddle cinches, graze his horses and eat something. The grass was good, and he could see for a long way in every direction. While he ate sandwiches of bread and cold bacon, he kept his eyes turned toward the mouth of the canyon, expecting to see men afoot come boiling out of it, carrying rifles. If he did, he was ready to get mounted and stay out of rifle range. Let them come. See how much gold ore they could carry in their pockets back to Cripple Creek. As Buck understood the law, they would have to prove that they had found some kind of valuable metal. If they didn't, their claims would soon be declared invalid.

Thinking of that brought a grin to Buck's face. Yeah, see how many rocks you can carry for a hundred and some odd miles. There's a lot of hills to climb between here and Cripple Creek. Those rocks are going to get mighty heavy. He hoped they suffered as much as he did.

But—the grin vanished—what had he accomplished? He'd put them afoot, but they were young and they could walk out. They could walk easier than he did. And they probably could carry enough ore to have it assayed. All Buck had done was make life miserable for them for a few days.

With no particular plan in mind, Buck tightened the cinches, mounted and rode back to the rim. Eyes peeled, he hobbled the horses and crept to the edge, carrying the 30-30. On his belly, he looked down. They were below him, across the creek, three of them, sitting on the ground eating out of tin cans. They didn't know yet their horses were gone. Weren't they going to be mad when they found out. They were well-supplied with a box of giant powder, shovels, picks, drill jacks and a sledge hammer. As far as they knew, there wasn't another human anywhere near.

Probably counting their wealth, Buck thought grimly. Talking about how they're going to spend the money they get for these claims. The one with the little smart-ass mustache, he'd probably been sleeping with Spooky's daughter. In fact, this whole scheme could have been his. Thinking about it made Buck's pulse race, his face hot, his mouth twist into an angry grimace. Just for that, you sonofabitch, I think I'll bounce a 30-30 slug off that rock you're sitting on.

The idea no more than popped into Buck's head when he was squinting down the rifle barrel. Take careful aim, he told himself. Don't want to kill him. Just make him jump.

KAPOW.

Jump, the man did. He jumped up so fast he had to have been stung on the ass. All three of them jumped. They looked at each other, looked up and down the canyon and finally up to the rim. Buck felt like waving his hat and yelling some kind of insult. Instead he put the rifle to his shoulder and fired again. He could see the bullet knock a piece off a rock in front of Dudley White.

"Jesus Christ," one of the men yelled. The words were faint by the time they reached Buck, but he understood them. Now they were moving. They grabbed up the rifles that had been leaning against a boulder and scrambled behind the same pile of low grade ore that Buck had once scrambled behind. They hadn't seen him yet, but if he fired another shot they would. He had to fire another shot — for revenge if nothing else. Taking aim at a tin can, Buck squeezed the trigger, watched the can bounce and roll downhill into the creek.

Hadigan's rifle was a good one. The long, bottle-shaped cartridges made a hell of a racket, but the lead slugs went where he aimed. Levering another round into the firing chamber, Buck looked down for another target.

But now he was seen and the men below were firing back. A bullet sang an angry song over Buck's head and another screamed off a rock only two feet away. He could see puffs of smoke from the rifle barrels and hear the shots two seconds later. Buck backed away from the rim.

What, he asked himself again, had he accomplished? He could have killed them. From up here he could have picked off two before they could take cover. But that would have made him a bushwhacker. Everybody hates a bushwhacker.

All right, Buck Innes, he said to himself, what

now?

If he was lucky he could keep them down there behind those rocks until dark, but that wouldn't accomplish anything either. All it would do, all he had done, was harass them. Give them a hard time. It wouldn't invalidate their claims on Spooky's mine. Shaking his head sadly, Buck knew there was no way he could do that short of killing them. He could try to run them out of the country, scare them into leaving their claims. But naw, there were three of them, well armed. Not much chance of that.

Well hell, now that he was here he might as well burn their asses a little bit, give them a dose of their own medicine. Looking back over the rim, he saw that one of the three was cautiously making his way across the creek while the other two stayed behind the rocks and watched for Buck. Buck fired. The man ran back to the rocks and jumped behind them. His partners fired back. Lead slugs sang, whistled and screamed past Buck's head. He pulled away from the edge, crawled twenty feet to another position and took another look down. They knew he had moved, but they hadn't spotted him yet. With his hat off and only his head showing, he would be hard to see until he fired.

"How do you like it, you sonsofbitches?" Buck muttered. "Too bad I can't start a flood."

An idea came to him. He couldn't start a flood, but he could create a hell of a big bang. Their box of giant powder was sitting out in the open, between the creek and the pile of rocks. He wondered how many sticks of powder were left in the box. Enough to blast a big hole in the canyon, maybe even divert the creek so it flooded Spooky's mine. The more Buck thought about the idea, the more he liked it. Yeah, blow up their dynamite so they'd have to do their digging with a pick and shovel. Make them work their asses off.

But—aw, hell. There was no way he could set off that powder from up here. Buck was no powder monkey but he had used the stuff to blast ice out of the creeks so cattle could drink. He knew how to use it. And he knew that bullets wouldn't set it off. Not even fire. In fact, he remembered a couple of cowboys arguing in a bunkhouse one night whether fire would explode dynamite. To settle the argument, one cowboy grabbed a stick of powder, opened the wood burning stove and tossed it inside. A half-dozen men were in the bunkhouse at the time. The bunkhouse was emptied in nothing flat. But the powder didn't explode.

No, it took a small explosion to set off the big one. That's what blasting caps were for.

Lying on his belly, peering over the edge, Buck looked for, and finally saw the small box of primer caps and a roll of fuse. The caps held a small amount of sensitive powder and a short sleeve for the fuse to fit into. It didn't take much to explode a cap. Careless men had lost fingers handling them. If the box of caps were on top of the box of dynamite, he could set off the caps with a rifle bullet, which might explode the giant powder. But it wasn't. It was a good three feet away on top of a small boulder. He'd have to settle for a small explosion.

Or would he? One stick of powder was on top of the boulder with the caps. It even had a fuse sticking out of it, and was ready to use. They'd been planning to put it in a hole they'd just drilled in the mine wall. One stick wouldn't blow up the world, but it would make a hell of a racket and scare the bejesus out of them. Another thing it would do: it would leave practically no trace of the primer caps, and without them the rest of their dynamite would be worthless. Yeah, it would do that much.

While he was mulling it over, one of the men below spotted him. Rifle bullets whined and screamed around him. He ducked immediately, and crawled back twenty feet to another spot.

Peering over the rim, Buck could see that the men below were watching the spot he'd just vacated. It would take careful aim to hit that small box of caps. He got the 30-30 to his shoulder, squinted down the barrel. They saw him. Bullets hit the dirt near him and sang over his head. One came so close to his face that he felt heat from it. One eye closed, he squinted down the rifle barrel with the other. Squeezed the trigger.

It was better than he'd hoped for. The caps exploded which exploded the stick of dynamite. Even as far away as Buck was the BOOM numbed his ears. Rocks and dirt flew fifty feet into the air, and that section of canyon was filled with dust so thick Buck couldn't see into it.

"Eat dirt, you sonsofbitches," Buck yelled. He got to his knees and watched as the dust slowly settled. A full minute went by, and Buck wondered if he'd killed the men. Then one staggered out from behind the pile of rocks. He was bareheaded, spitting dust. Another crawled out, then stood, swaying like a drunk man. The third one came out coughing and spitting, wiping his eyes with a shirt sleeve.

They weren't hurt, but for the moment at least they didn't know up from down or sideways.

Chapter Twenty

A grin turned up the corners of Buck's mouth as he looked down at them. They weren't trying to spot him now, only trying to stop their heads from splitting and their ears from ringing.

Maybe it was time to go. He'd done all he could to get even with them without killing or crippling them. Glancing at the sky, he figured it was about two hours until dark. But damnit he'd ridden a long ways to harass these three, and he couldn't leave yet. Exactly, what else he could do, he didn't know. Maybe stay where he was and fire a shot now and then to keep them in the canyon a little longer. Make them search in the dark for their horses and spend the night trying to figure out what happened to them.

Picking still a different spot, Buck lay on his belly and watched. They were sitting on boulders now, hacking and coughing. Finally, one walked on unsteady legs to the creek and splashed water on his face. The others followed. They washed their faces, coughed and spat, then went looking for their hats. Buck watched them search through the rubble for their guns, find them, stand around for a few minutes as if deciding what to do, then start walking down the creek.

KAPOW. Buck fired another shot at the ground in front of the leading man. He stopped so suddenly one of the others ran into him. They looked up at the canyon rim, looked at each other, then hurried back to their mine dump fortress. For several long moments, they were afraid to show their heads. Then as Buck squinted down at them, a white rag, probably a handkerchief, tied to the end of a rifle barrel was shoved up from behind the rocks. It was waved from side to side. Next a man raised his face above the rocks, cupped his mouth with his hands and yelled something. Buck didn't understand what. The man tried again:

"WHAT . . . WANT?" His voice echoed up and down the canyon.

It was a good question. What do I want, Buck asked himself. I want them plumb out of the country, that's what I want, but there's no way I can make them git. The man yelled again, "WHAT . . . WANT? WHO . . ."

Who am I? Why, I'm Spooky Hallows, that's who I am. Buck cupped his hands around his mouth and yelled down, "I'M THE GHOST OF SPOOKY HALLOWS. THAT'S MY MINE. YOU AIN'T WELCOME."

"WHAT?"

Buck yelled the same message, yelled as loud as he could. And after a lifetime of hollering at cattle, he could yell.

The face below ducked behind the rock dump. Long moments passed. The face appeared again. "WHAT . . . WANT?"

"I WANT YOU GONE. GIT, OR I'LL HAUNT YOU 'TILL YOU DO."

181

". . . LEGAL CLAIM."

"I'M A GHOST. LEGAL DON'T MEAN NOTHIN'."

All was quiet. The three were talking it over. Time passed. Buck glanced again at the sky. A dark cloud had drifted under the sun, but it didn't look threatening. The face appeared.

"WHO . . . YOU?"

"SPOOKY'S GHOST. I'M HERE TO HAUNT YOU."

Quiet again. Then:

"WE . . . DONE NOTHIN' . . . YOU."

"THAT'S MY MINE. GIT."

More silence. The sun was out again, moving closer to the horizon. It was taking the three a while to decide what to say next, or do next.

Time passed. Then:

"WE'LL GO . . . DON'T SHOOT."

Sure, Buck thought. Sure, you'll go 'till you get out of that trap you're in. Then all promises are broken. All bets are off. He cast another glance at the sky. It wouldn't be long until dark. All right, let them go. He couldn't keep them in there after dark anyway. Without answering, he backed away from the rim, stood and went to his horses.

Yep, he thought as he tightened cinches and got mounted, they'll wait a while to be sure I'm gone, then they'll walk out of the canyon. Then they'll cuss and run off in all directions looking for their horses. By morning they'll know they're afoot. That's when they'll come lookin' for me.

"Yep," he said aloud, "it's time to go."

Buck Innes still had no plan. He rode back to the creek, took a drink of water, watered his horses, mounted again and turned east toward Cripple Creek, trying to think of something. He'd never killed a man. Sure, he'd been shot at and missed, shot at and hit, and he'd fired a few shots at Indians, cattle rustlers, and now these gents, but he'd never killed anyone. In a gunfight, with someone trying to kill him, he'd shoot to kill too. He had no doubt about that. But he couldn't just stand back where it was safe, take aim at a man's chest and kill him. That was where those three gunnies had an advantage. They wouldn't hesitate a second to kill. They'd kill a man from ambush or in a fight. It didn't matter to them. All that mattered was whether they'd gain anything by it.

So if Buck wanted to kill the three — without answering to his conscience and the law — he had to get them in a fight where the odds were on their side. And that, he grinned wryly, would be suicide. In a fair fight the best he could hope for was to get two of them. Not all three. No one could be that lucky. Even if he did, no one would believe it. A trial jury wouldn't believe it. No, but they could kill him, hide his body and go on about their business. He'd just disappear the way Spooky did. Maybe one day his bones would be found, but by then those three would have sold their claims and be long gone.

Buck could do that to them, too, and pretend he knew nothing about them. But he wasn't that kind, and it wouldn't work anyway. Spooky's daughter knew the three were coming back to Shotgun Canyon, and Hadigan knew Buck was coming back too. And there were others who knew — George Hinson, for one. It wouldn't be easy to hide three bodies, and if the hoodlums were found shot, Buck would be the first one the law looked for.

183

These were the thoughts that went through Buck's mind as he rode east. "Aw hell," he grumbled aloud. "Damn and god damn." He wished he'd never got into this mess. He wished he'd never met Spooky's daughter. Were it not for her, he wouldn't be here. That got him to thinking about something else: Spooky's daughter and Dudley White. Both were from Denver. Somehow they'd got together and cooked up a scheme to find either her dad or her dad's mine. And they'd used Buck Innes to help them do it. What's more they intended to kill Buck when they found the mine. Spooky too, if he was there. They wanted the whole thing to themselves. Kill her own dad?

Boy, did he want to see her again. He had plenty to say to her. He wondered if she was back in Cripple Creek yet. Suddenly, he had a powerful urge to get back to town as soon as he could.

Then what?

Oh, he'd bawl her out and tell her what he thought of her, but what good would it do? She held a claim to Spooky's mine and there was no way he could take it away from her.

Hurry back? What for? Just to be reminded of what a damned fool he was? For the rest of his life, every time he heard about Spooky's mine, or the Shotgun Mine, or whatever it was called in the future, he'd be reminded.

Buck Innes was in a sour mood when he camped that night. He reckoned he was a good five miles east of Shotgun Canyon. The three gunhands wouldn't start their long walk until next morning, after they'd discovered for certain that they had to walk. Horses hobbled and grazing, he built a fire among some lodgepole pines, boiled some coffee, unwrapped the last of his steaks, smelled of it, threw it away and opened a tin of dried beef. The old ache was back as he sat on the ground and ate. It kept him awake most of the night.

The sky was cloudy in the west when Buck crawled stiffly out of his blankets. But blue sky showed itself on the eastern horizon, and maybe the sun would shine. Maybe it wouldn't. It might rain like a cow unloading on a rock. It might be a hot dry day. Who knows? "Who cares, anyway," Buck muttered. He'd long ago learned to carry a rain slicker behind the cantle every time he got on a horse. The slicker had saved him a lot of chills.

He took his time checking the horses, building a fire, boiling some coffee, frying some bacon. Smoke from the fire would be seen by the three gunnies, but what difference did it make? He'd stay far enough ahead of them on the way back to Cripple Creek that they'd be wasting ammunition trying to put a bullet in him. Maybe he'd even fire a shot at them now and then, just to make more problems. He wished he'd stolen their chuck when he had a chance. They ought to be going hungry the way he did.

He ate his breakfast out of the skillet so he'd have less dish-washing to do, grumbled and groused about the old bullet wound in his hip, and caught his horses. He was pulling the lash cinch tight on the pack horse when he saw riders coming.

At the sight of riders, Buck stiffened, then hurried to his saddle horse and pulled the 30-30 out of its scabbard. There were two of them and they were coming from the east, not from Shotgun Canyon. Standing with the rifle loaded and cocked, Buck watched them come. They had seen his smoke and now they had seen him, and they were coming, riding at a walk. When they got closer, he could see that their horses were carrying more than saddle horses ought to carry. Besides saddles and men, they had blanket rolls, picks and shovels, an axe, a skillet and a coffee pot, all tied on the saddles. It took a lot of rope to tie that much stuff on the sides, fronts and backs of the saddles.

Before they came within rifle range, they stopped and waved. They appeared to be friendly. Prospectors. No doubt looking for Shotgun Canyon. Buck let the hammer down on the 30-30, and pointed it at the ground. The riders came on then.

"Well, I'll be gone to hell," one of them said, grinning a wide grin. "You're the feller that fed me a while back. Remember me?"

"Yeah," Buck said, grinning with him, "your name is, uh, Harvey. Yeah, I remember you. Looks like you got your stake."

"Can we git down?" William Harvey asked. "We walk and lead these horses half the time. They're carryin' too much of a load."

"Sure, get down. I just broke camp or I'd have some coffee on."

"We done et. Meet my new partner, Jack Herschel." Both men dismounted.

"How do," the other man said.

William Harvey was healthier than he was the first time Buck had seen him, and he had only two days growth of whiskers. His clothes were new and he still carried the old hogleg pistol on his hip. His partner was thin, but wiry, with a prominent adam's apple and a wide-brimmed black hat on his head. Their horses looked to be in good shape.

"Bet I can guess where you're headed," Buck said.

186

William Harvey's grin widened. "We heered all about it. You and the young lady that was with you didn't find her pa, but you found his mine. A place called Shotgun Canyon. I been driftin' all over this country lookin' for color, and I seen a lot of canyons, but I ain't seen that one."

"How did you know where to look?"

"Wal, I recollected where I seen you and the lady, and I knowed which direction you was headed, and I figure that mine has to be somewhere around about here."

"Did we figure right?" asked Jack Herschel.

"You keep goin' due west and you'll fall into it."

"Hot damn," said William Harvey, slapping his right thigh. "I knowed I could find 'er." He turned to his partner. "Tole you I could. You didn't waste your money when you staked me."

Shaking his head, Buck said, "I hope you're not too late. Four people've got claims around that mine."

William Harvey continued grinning. "That's what we heered in the county gover'ment office. But four people can't claim the whole country, and where's there's one vein there's another'n, and we aim to find 'er and stake out our own claims before ever'body else finds 'er."

"A lot of men are lookin'," said Jack Herschel.

"I know about that," Buck said. "Say, have you ever heard of a man named Shoemaker?"

"Shoemaker? Hmm." Harvey looked down and rubbed his chin. "Don't rec'lect any Shoemaker. How about you, Jack?"

"No. Well, maybe. Met a feller on a train once. 'Bout a year ago. I b'lieve he said his name was Shoemaker."

187

"On the train from Florence?"

"Naw, from Colorado City up to Florissant. We got to jawin' to pass the time. Come to think of it I never saw 'im again when we got off the train. I took the stage on down to Cripple Creek."

"Who's he?" Harvey asked.

"I don't know. Another gold hunter, I reckon. Thought you might of run into 'im."

"I b'lieve he said his name was Shoemaker."

"What did he look like?"

Jack Herschel squinted at the horizon thoughtfully. "I disremember, exactly. All I remember is he was a workin' man, not one of them city dandies."

"Whoever he is," said William Harvey, "if he's huntin' color, he'll be along sooner or later." Smiling, he added, "So she's right over yonder, is she? Damn, I can't wait to see 'er."

"Well good luck to you," Buck said. Then another thought came to his mind. Frowning, shaking his head, he said, "Listen, fellers, there's three gunslingers over there, and they're madder than a crow on a wet nest. Their horses are gone and they're afoot, and they're ready to kill anybody they can get in their rifle sights. They need horses, and they'll kill you to get yours. Keep your eyes peeled and keep the hell away from them."

The smile left Harvey's face. "We heered about them three. We heered they was hardcases." He slapped the holster on his right hip. "I've got this here Rocky Mountain howitzer and Jack's got a Winchester repeatin' gun. We ain't lettin' 'em keep us out."

Still frowning, Buck said, "They tried to kill me. Don't give 'em a chance. They'll bushwhack you or sneak up on you in the dark. They'd cut your throats for a dollar, and they'd cut your heads off for them horses."

"We'll keep our eyes open. Straight west, you say?"

Buck watched them go. He watched until they were out of sight. By then the sun was two hours above the eastern horizon, and the clouds were burning off. Finally, Buck mounted and turned his horses toward the sun.

He hadn't traveled five hundred yards when he heard the gunshots.

Chapter Twenty-one

There were two shots at first, away off in the distance. Two muffled POPs. Then another. Now there was a volley of shots. Buck reined up and listened. One more POP, then silence.

Buck muttered, "Holy jumpin' . . . Somebody sure as hell shot somebody. I warned them fellers. Hope they made a fair fight out of it."

What should he do? Go back and help the two prospectors? Yeah, and maybe ride right into an ambush. The shooting had stopped. The damage was done. Whoever was shot was shot. Buck could only hope it wasn't the prospectors. They seemed like decent fellers. But he knew they'd been ambushed. Sure, as hell they'd been killed.

Now the killers had horses. Two horses, anyway. Unless Harvey and Herschel had managed to get in a few shots and make them count, two of the three would be coming after Buck. But the gold hunters on horses were the best targets, and if anyone survived it wasn't them. They were down and dead, that's all there was to it. Two killers on horses weren't as dangerous as three, but when the lead started flying again, Buck wanted a fair chance. He had to ride, find a place to fort up.

Glancing around, he could see no kind of cover for at least a mile. The little grove of lodgepoles he'd camped in wasn't much, but it would be better than nothing. Or would it? There was nothing in there to take cover behind, and the trees would make it easier for a man to sneak up on him. Ride. Get as near a hill or a gulley as he could.

Buck started to kick his saddle horse in the sides. Hesitated. A rider was coming. Fogging it. A shovel, an axe and every damned thing were flapping and beating on the horse as it ran as hard as it could. Buck got down with the 30-30 in his hands. He dropped to one knee and got the rider in his sights.

"Hey-ay-ay," the rider yelled. Screamed, rather.

Buck let the hammer down on the 30-30. It was Jack Herschel, bareheaded, hair flying in the wind, whipping the horse with the end of the bridle reins.

"Hey-ay-ay." He rode up, pulled the horse to a stop with both hands. His face was white and his eyes were wild. "They shot Bill. They killed 'im. They just jumped up from somewhere in the grass and started shootin'."

"Aw, for cryin' out loud."

"My horse boogered when they jumped up, and they missed me. I saw Bill fall off his horse. He was dead. Wasn't nothin' I could do for 'im."

"Three of 'em?"

"Yeah."

"So now they've got Bill's horse."

"Yeah. They'd of got me if this horse hadn't stampeded. It was all I could do to hang on 'im. I just let 'im run 'till he got winded and then I whipped 'im to keep 'im goin'."

"Well, that leads the goddam parade."

"What?"

"What you'd better do, mister, is untie all that junk from your saddle and get ready to fight."

"Fight? I can't fight. My goddamn gun jammed. I tried to shoot back at 'em while I was ridin', and my goddamn gun jammed."

"Where is it?"

"I dropped it. I had to hang onto this hammer-headed horse."

"Well, I've got two guns. I'll loan you my sixgun. They've got one horse so there won't be more'n one of 'em comin' after us."

"I'm ridin'. I'm headin' for town and the shurff. Those crazy outfits killed my partner."

"It's two days to town. That horse ain't gonna make it the way you're travelin'."

Jack Herschel cast a fearful look behind him, then dismounted. Buck helped him untie a shovel and an axe from the saddle. That left only a blanket roll and, Buck hoped, some chuck rolled up in the blankets.

"If you're smart, Mister Innes, you'll head for town too."

"I ain't runnin' from 'em. I had to run from 'em once when there was three of 'em. I ain't runnin' now. I can shoot as good as any of 'em."

"I'm ridin'. I ain't never shot a man and I ain't gonna." With that, Jack Herschel climbed on his horse, kicked it in the sides and whipped it with the bridle reins.

Buck yelled after him. "It's a long ways. Save your horse." He doubted Jack Herschel heard him.

Mounted, Buck rode east, following the fleeing man, but not trying to catch him. Instead he rode at a slow trot, looking for a place to fort up. He kept a watch behind him. The only trees in sight were the ones he'd just left, but he'd already decided that that was not a good place to take a stand in a gun fight. He had no doubt that one of the three gunhands would be coming, trying to catch Jack Herschel, kill him and take his horse. The gunnies knew Herschel was unarmed. One of them would be coming any minute now.

No hurry, Buck told himself. Find a gulley or something. Save your horses. Too bad that Herschel feller don't have more guts. Probably took off at the first shot and left his partner dead. Maybe that's the only thing he could do. But he should have stayed with me. One gunslinger is nothing to fear. If there were two of us, that one'd have somethin' to fear himself.

Looking back, Buck saw the one man riding hard toward him.

There wasn't a gulley anywhere. A shallow draw stretched north and south about two hundred yards ahead. Too shallow. A low hill rose beyond the draw. Buck kicked his saddle horse and got both horses into a lope. Looking back, he could see the man gaining on him. The hill was just ahead. Buck rode up it at a gallop, dismounted on the run, felt a sharp pain in the old hip wound, and hit the ground on his belly.

The way the rider was coming, he'd be within rifle range in ten seconds. Buck crawled away from his horses and lay flat again. No use getting the horses shot.

Squinting down the rifle barrel, Buck waited. "Just come a little closer," he muttered. But the rider pulled up. He sat his horse and stared at Buck. "Come on," Buck said. The rider didn't come on. Instead, he dismounted, knelt on one knee, put a rifle to his shoulder and fired. A puff of smoke came out of the rifle barrel long before the sound reached Buck. The bullet fell short. The rifleman jumped back on the horse and started riding around Buck.

"Aw, for cryin' in the kitchen," Buck grumbled. "He

don't want no fight with me. He wants that other feller, the man that dropped his gun. Might get 'im too. Anybody'd that'd drop his gun in a gunfight ain't very smart." So what was Buck going to do? Just stand there and do nothing? Damned if he would.

The 30-30 didn't have the range that the new hunting rifles had, but it would shoot farther than a .44-40. Buck shifted positions, got his left elbow on his left knee to steady the rifle barrel. Lead him a little, he told himself. Aim a little high for distance. Steady.

POW.

He felt the recoil against his right cheek and shoulder. Immediately, he levered in another round. It wasn't necessary. The man continued riding for two seconds, then pitched forward onto the horse's neck and rolled off. He hit the ground so hard he bounced. The horse kept on running.

For a few seconds Buck couldn't believe it. "Lord," he said aloud, looking at the rifle in his hands, turning it, admiring it. Old Hadigan knew what he was doing when he bought this gun. If this one could shoot that far, how far could those new bolt action hunting rifles shoot?

Was that man over there dead or did he get scared and fall off his horse? Only one way to find out. Buck walked toward him, cautiously, the rifle cocked and ready to fire from the hip. The man lay sprawled on his back, arms and legs spreadeagled. He didn't move, and when Buck got close enough he knew why. The 30-30 slug had hit him in the right side of the head. The head was now shaped like a big egg, and blood was slowly running from a gaping wound in the temple into the ear. The eyes were open, sightless.

"Lord."

This wasn't Dudley White. This was either James Butcher or Benjamin Gotswald. It didn't matter much. He was a lifeless piece of . . .

And suddenly, for some reason that Buck Innes didn't understand, his hands started shaking and his legs felt weak. He wanted to sit down, he wanted to bawl like a baby. He mumbled, "What's the matter with me?" The dead man's misshapen head, his eyes, held a terrible fascination. Just a few minutes ago this was a healthy young man, and now he was nothing but a lifeless, bleeding hunk of something dead. And Buck had done it. He'd killed a man.

He sat. He put the rifle on the ground and sat with his knees drawn up and his arms and head on his knees. He couldn't stop his hands from trembling.

Finally, ordering himself to breathe deeply, he stopped trembling and began to think. "What the hell's the matter with you, Buck? You've shot deer, elk, coyotes and bears. This thing here had no more right to live than they did."

Standing, still forcing himself to breathe in deep breaths, he studied the terrain around him. Nothing but the horses moved anywhere. The dead man's horse was standing with its head down, sides heaving, about a hundred yards away. Buck's horses were cropping the grass on top of the hill. "Huh," Buck snorted aloud. This horse belonged to William Harvey. This piece of crud here had killed William Harvey and now Buck had killed him. All right, go on about your business, Buck Innes. No, you can't go yet, you've got to do something with the body. Can't just leave it here for the coyotes and wolves to feed on. What?

He had no shovel to dig a grave, and it would take a lot of rocks to cover a dead man, more rocks than Buck could gather in a few hours. Just leave him here for his partners to find? Maybe they wouldn't find him. They wouldn't be packing a shovel anyway. With his head down, Buck walked back to his horses, trying

195

to figure out what to do.

Mounted, leading his pack horse, he rode to the dead man's horse, leaned out of the saddle and picked up the reins, then rode back to the body. He hated to give up the bed tarp he'd had for more years than he wanted to remember, but he couldn't leave the dead man exposed. He unrolled his bed and separated the blankets and mattress from the tarp. Trying not to look at the body, he put the arms at its sides and its feet together and rolled it up in the tarp. Then he noticed the hat lying upside down nearby. Swearing under his breath, he unrolled the body, put the hat on top of its face, and rolled it up again. He had to strain and grunt to pick up the dead man and got him onto the cross-buck saddle on the pack horse. The dead man's head was on one side of the saddle and his legs were on the other side. Buck tied each end to the lash cinch. The remainder of his bed he rolled up and tied across the saddle on the dead man's horse.

There was the rifle, the dead man's rifle. Buck picked it up. It was a Winchester .44-40. A good gun in its day, but no match for the new 30-30s. Buck shoved it into a boot on the extra horse's saddle, tied the horse to the crossbuck saddle, and was ready to go.

Half-expecting to see men running toward him on foot, he took another long look to the west, saw nothing, and rode away.

It was past mid-afternoon when Buck saw what he was looking for—a long, rocky ridge with boulders strewn about as if by a giant hand. The ridge could be seen for a half-dozen miles, and one of the boulders was as high as a horse. It stuck up above everything else. That was what Buck headed for. When he got there, he lifted the body off the pack horse. Then lifting, pushing with his shoulder and cussing, he got it on top of the boulder. It lay up there, wrapped like a mummy, but easy to recognize as a human body.

Now the coyotes and wolves couldn't get to it and the magpies — those big black and white carrion-eating birds — couldn't peck through the heavy bed tarp. It was the best Buck could do. It was still almost two days to Cripple Creek, and he'd be damned if he was going to camp with that dead man. Not only that, rigor mortis would set in by morning, and he'd have had a hell of a time tying a stiff body on a horse. No, this was the best thing to do. By the time Deputy John Burghart, or anybody, found it rigor mortis would have left and it would be easier to move.

Looking back as he rode away, now leading two horses, Buck mumbled sourly, "Doo dah."

Chapter Twenty-two

As hungry as he was, he had to ride out of sight of the boulder and the dead man before he stopped to eat. The horses rested and grazed while he sat under a ponderosa and ate out of a can. He couldn't help glancing repeatedly to the west, toward Shotgun Canyon. What would Dudley White and the other gunsel do? Wait most of the day for their partner to come back, or start walking? Either way, Buck was safe. They wouldn't catch up. Still, he couldn't help feeling a little nervous and watching his back trail. At the same time, he wondered how far the prospector Jack Herschel had traveled. The way he was riding, he'd be far ahead. The gunfight, as brief as it was, and having to dispose of a dead body had slowed Buck down. He'd be doing well if he got back to Cripple Creek tomorrow night. Jack Herschel, if his horse didn't die first, would get there far ahead of him.

Two hours before sundown, Buck had to stop. He'd traveled as far as he could that day. For several miles he'd been walking and leading the three horses, trying to ease the pain in his hip. The pain wouldn't go away. There was no water where he stopped, but the horses had been watered in a creek a few hours earlier, and Buck had spent the night in dry camps before. Without water for coffee, he made his meal out of tinned beef and a can of peaches. The syrup in the peach can gave him enough moisture to keep his throat from drying up.

It was hours after he'd crawled into his blankets that he finally went to sleep. At first he thought about the man he'd killed. The man was a killer himself, but he was some mother's son. Was his mother alive? Would she wonder what had become of her boy? Did the dead man have any brothers and sisters? Did he have any papers in his pockets that would identify him?

"Lord," Buck muttered. Then a more pleasant thought came to his mind: the three men who'd tried to kill him—who'd killed William Harvey—would be hunted as killers now. Harvey's partner, Jack Herschel, would get to Cripple Creek and report the murder. They would be arrested or hunted. Their mining claims would be abandoned. Buck got some satisfaction out of that. But not much.

Others would grab the claims. Sooner or later and probably sooner, others would find Shotgun Canyon and Spooky's mine. It was only a matter of time until claims would be marked all over that territory.

Well, Spooky's daughter had the best claim. She didn't deserve it, but who else did? Buck Innes? Naw. All Buck wanted to do was get back to Mrs. Davenport's boarding house and rest his bones. Let the damned miners and prospectors fight it out. No, on second thought there was one other thing he wanted to do, he wanted a chance to tell Spooky's daughter what he thought of her. He wished she were a man so he could take a gun butt to her. Yeah, he wanted to do that.

He shifted positions about a hundred times that night, trying to ease the ache. Finally he slept.

When he woke up the sun was shining in his face. He jumped up and looked around wildly. How could he have slept so late? Was he that tired? Or was it because he had lain awake so long? Thank God nobody was in

199

sight and the horses were grazing peacefully only a short distance away. It was a good time of day for grazing, early, before the flies were bad. Buck limped around in a circle for a while to get the stiffness out of his hips and legs, then rummaged through his pack panniers for something to eat. He settled for some stale bread and a can of beans. "Gaw-wk," he said as he forced it down. The horses were faring better than he was.

Throughout the day he rode and walked alternately. And every ten minutes or so he looked back. Still nothing human in sight. He mounted and rode up the hills then dismounted and walked down. He crossed grassy valleys and rocky ridges. He pushed through buck brush, low tree limbs and willows. At noon he built a fire and made coffee. No use starving himself. But he knew he wasn't as close to Cripple Creek as he'd expected to be, and he was worried that he'd have to spend another night sleeping on the ground. After eating, he splashed water on his face from a trickle of a stream. Running his hands over his face he remembered he hadn't shaved since leaving Cripple Creek a long time ago. It seemed like a long time ago. He reckoned his face and head looked like a porcupine.

By mid-afternoon he knew he wasn't going to make it to town that day. He'd had to walk and stop to rest too often. He hadn't seen any sign of anyone behind him, and he guessed that Dudley White and his partner had waited most of the day before they started walking. But in case he'd guessed wrong, he made another smokeless camp and rolled out his bed in a shallow ravine. The 30-30 was leaning against a rock beside his bed and the Colt Peacemaker was under the blankets with him.

Again, he didn't sleep well. He vowed that from this night on he was through sleeping on the ground. He'd earned his right to a bed on springs, and he by God wasn't going to settle for anything less. And no more meals cooked over an open fire. And for sure no more meals that hadn't even been cooked. If Mrs. Davenport ever opened one of these damned hermetically sealed cans, he would refuse to eat what came out of it.

Buck Innes, he promised himself, when you get back to town you're gonna retire for good.

Buck. How did he get that name anyway? Reaching back into his memory — away back — he recalled one of the hired hands calling him Buckaroo as a joke. He was only four or five. His dad had made him a catch rope out of a length of cotton clothesline, and he'd tried to lasso everything he could get close enough to. Little Buckaroo, the hired man had called him. Buckaroos were a different breed of cowboys who ranged farther north — where that hired man had drifted from — so the nickname was shortened to Buck. Yeah, that's how it was. The name Buck had stuck to him ever since. He even signed his name Buck Innes. After his mother died, his real name, Hiram, was almost forgotten.

Buck Innes was sore and stiff when he rolled out at the crack of dawn next morning. After walking some of the soreness out and studying the country to the west he built a fire and had coffee, bacon and beans. Then before the sun came up he was horseback and starting the last dozen miles to town. The whole sorry mess, his part of it anyhow, would soon be over. The rest would be up to the deputy sheriff. It would be interesting.

Buck would sit on the boarding house porch and watch and he would go to the Royal Flush saloon and listen. Unless Dudley White and partner were foot racers they would be caught and arrested for murder. There would be a trial. Buck and Jack Herschel would be the main witnesses. The whole town would turn out. The shuffle and hassle of settling mining claims in and around Shotgun Canyon would be something else to watch. Some claims would be settled by gunfire, and

201

some would be settled by lawyers. The lawyers would profit without digging and scratching in the rocks, without even getting their hands dirty. Some men would get rich and some would lose their asses and all the fixtures. Buck would be an observer.

Yep, it was going to be something.

He had just ridden out of the timber west of the cemetery when he saw riders coming. There were five men, headed in his general direction but a little south. When they saw him they changed directions and came toward him at a high trot.

"Buck," said Deputy Burghart, "I might of known you'd survive. How in hell are you?"

Grinning, Buck said, "Finer'n the fur on a cat's ass. You gents're packin' enough artillery to take on Pancho Villa. Are you headed where I think you are?"

Besides Deputy Burghart, there were Jack Herschel on a fresh horse, and three men whom Buck had seen around town. Each man was carrying a repeating rifle and a sixgun. They didn't talk long. Deputy Burghart was eager to get after some murderers. Buck told them where they could find the body of one, and he told how the man was killed. The deputy got Buck's promise to feed him all the details when the posse returned.

"I'll be more'n happy to oblige you, sheriff," Buck said. He added, "But don't stray too far south." He pointed in the direction they should be going. "Aim straight that way and you'll pick up their sign. I'm bettin' they won't be hard to find."

They were gone, riding at a high trot.

The old wound in his right hip was throbbing when Buck rode past the cemetery and into the outskirts of Cripple Creek. In spite of his whiskers and the weary way he sat his saddle, no one paid much attention to him. Prospectors and travelers were riding into town all the time. They came from everywhere. Not even the horse carrying an empty saddle drew much attention. Buck headed straight for Hinson's barn, his three horses clip-clopping on the hard-packed streets.

On a whim, he decided to stop at Spooky's one-room cabin, just on the small chance the old prospector was there. He knew he wouldn't be, but he had to ride past the cabin anyway. The gate to Spooky's small pasture was still open, and the cabin door was open a few inches. Buck dismounted sorely and opened it further, looked inside. Nothing had changed. He was trying to decide whether to get horseback or walk and lead the horses the rest of the way when he spotted the pile of rocks beside the cabin. He remembered seeing them before. It would be easier to walk, he was thinking, but damnit, he'd been a cattleman and everyone knew that cattlemen never walked when they could ride. Buck wasn't going to tell anyone about walking and leading his horses and he wasn't going to be seen doing it. Getting back on the horse with his crippled hip would be painful, but he was going to ride.

The rocks reminded him of something.

Buck paused with one foot in the stirrup, paused and tried to think. He dropped the reins and walked over to the rocks. Looked down at them. Kicked them. Picked one up and studied it. It was granite with a light streak through it. Maybe it was a streak of quartz or maybe it was that pyrite he'd heard about, a mineral sometimes called fool's gold.

Buck stared at it without seeing it. Something was pulling at his mind, pulling hard. He tried to think. His brain was working, straining. Something was whispering to him now, whispering a message he couldn't quite understand. He mumbled, "It ain't right. It's all wrong. What's wrong? What?" Trying to concentrate, he stared blankly at the horizon, stared at the ground, frowned, cleared his throat.

203

And suddenly he groaned, "Oh-h-h. You don't think
. . . oh-h-h."

Sitting on the ground, cross-legged, he let out another, "Oh-h-h. It can't be. It can. Good Lord a-mighty.
Oh-h-h."

Then he began to laugh. At first it came out as more
of a whimper than a laugh, then it changed to a giggle,
then finally to a guffaw. He laughed until tears rolled
down his cheeks. He laughed until he was weak with
laughter. He fell back and rolled over on his side, laugh-
ing. The more he thought about it the more he laughed.
He laughed until his sides hurt.

Still chuckling, he stood and went to his horses, got
his left foot in the stirrup and crawled awkwardly and
sorely into the saddle. Horseback, leading two horses,
he chuckled all the way to Hinson's barn, not seeing
anyone, not seeing anything. At the barn, George Hinson stopped raking manure long enough to stare and
say:

"Buck, what the hell's so damned funny?"

Between chuckles, Buck said only, "Aw nothin'."

"Somethin's sure tickled your funny bone."

"You ain't gonna believe it."

"Ain't gonna believe what?"

"Aw nothin'."

"Well, where'd you get that other horse? That was my
horse 'till I sold 'im. What become of the feller I sold 'im
to?"

Thinking of the man he'd killed wiped the smile off
Buck's face. "He's dead. He was a killer and he got
killed."

"What? I heered about a killin' away over west somewheres. Was he part of that?"

"Yeah."

"What happened?"

"Tell you about it later." And Buck's smile returned, a

smile, then a giggle then a guffaw.

"Well, when you git over your haw-hawin' you better go see that young woman, that Anita Hallows."

The smile disappeared again. "Anita Hallows? She's back in town?"

"She sure as hell is and she wants to see you. She's been over here ever' day for the last three-four days to find out if you and some others've come back yet."

"She has?"

"Yup. She's been lookin' for you and a gent named White and some other gents named Butcher or somethin'."

"Well, I'll be damned."

"She's stayin' at the Palace."

With jaws clenched, Buck unsaddled and turned the horses out into Hinson's pasture. Leaving his belongings in Hinson's barn, he turned his steps toward Bennett Avenue and the Palace Hotel.

"You goin' over to see her?"

"You damned betcha," Buck said over his shoulder. He added, mostly to himself, "Right now there ain't anybody in the world I want to see more than I want to see her."

Chapter Twenty-three

In spite of the pain in his hip, Buck Innes walked with rapid steps over the path and through the tall grass to Meyers Avenue. He crossed that street without even seeing other pedestrians, then limped uphill on the rocky road to Bennett Avenue. The Palace Hotel was in the next block. Boots thumping on the boardwalk, Buck threaded his way between miners, bankers, lawyers, gamblers and well-dressed ladies. He didn't hear the noise from creaking freight wagons. He didn't hear the steam whistles at the mines. All he could think about was her.

She was there, in the hotel dining room, sitting alone at a table for four, eating a late breakfast and sipping coffee, looking innocent and prissy. Her blond hair was brushed and shiny, and her long gray and white dress was spotless. Her blue eyes opened wide in surprise when she saw Buck bearing down on her.

"I want to talk to you," Buck said loud enough for everyone in the room to hear.

She glanced around at the other customers, embarrassed at the attention Buck was drawing. The dining room was elegant with fine silverware, crystal water pitchers and linen tablecloths. His dirty clothes and stubby gray whiskers didn't belong there.

"Do you want to talk in here or someplace private?" He stood before her with his hands on his hips.

"Well, I, uh, I suppose we can . . ." She glanced around again, then averted her eyes.

"Your room or right here or out on the street. It don't matter to me."

Standing, eyes still averted, she said, "Well, we can go to my room to talk privately, if you wish."

"I damn well wish," Buck said.

She led the way up the stairs, back straight, holding her skirts above her ankles with one hand. Buck followed, and for a second admired her rump, but only for a second. At her door, she produced a key from a small silk purse and inserted it in the lock. With a quick look up and down the hall, she opened the door and stepped inside. Buck followed and stood in the center of the room with his hands on his hips.

The room was well-furnished with lacy curtains on the window, a hand-carved wooden headboard for the bed, an oak chiffonier and an armoire that reached the ceiling. A ladies comb and hand mirror lay on the chiffonier along with a box of face powder and a few scattered hairpins.

Once the door was closed, her soft gentle face turned hard. "Where's Dudley? Mr. White?"

"Oh, I wouldn't wait for him, Miss Hallows." Buck shifted his weight from one foot to the other and hooked his thumbs inside his gun belt. "He's either runnin' from the law or on his way back to town wearin' handcuffs. Or soon will be."

The hard look was replaced by a worry frown. "Why? What happened?"

"A lot happened. Your lover boy and his sidekicks tried to kill me, remember? Well, they finally got to kill somebody. Remember a sourdough named William Harvey? They killed him. The sheriff and four other men are hot after them."

"I . . . I don't believe it."

"How can you not believe it. You saw 'em try to kill me. While I was tryin' to save your bacon they was blazin' away at me. In fact, I think you tried to help 'em."

"Oh no," she said, backing away. "I didn't mean . . . they said they only wanted to find the mine. They didn't say they would . . . oh no, I didn't mean for that to happen." She dropped heavily onto the bed and sat with her hands in her lap.

"You sure as hell didn't try to stop 'em."

"I couldn't. I . . . couldn't stop them. I thought you had drowned in all that water that came out of the canyon. I, we, brought your things back to town."

"Sure, you wanted it to look like I was killed in an accident and you were only doin' what you could for the deceased."

She was silent now, staring at the floor.

"I can guess how it happened. That dandy, your lover boy, came to Cripple Creek to see what all the excitement was about and heard about your dad havin' a rich mine someplace. Everybody in Cripple Creek knew about your dad. Lover Boy went back to Denver and cooked up a scheme. You came here pretendin' to look for your dad, but you was really only interested in findin' his mine. You used me to find it for you, and they followed."

208

With pain in her eyes, she looked up at Buck. "We meant no harm to anyone."

"S'pose old Spooky, er Andy, was alive. What then?"

"We were going to take care of him, see that he had enough to live out his years."

"Is that what your lover boy told you?"

"Yes."

"He's a damned liar and you're a damned fool."

Unable to meet his gaze, she looked down again. "Perhaps I . . . perhaps I am."

"How come you left town right after you got back?"

"Dudley, Mr. White, wanted me to. We filed claims and he wanted me out of town for a while to be certain that I didn't let it slip where the mine is. He said men would find out about the mine and try to trick me into giving away the location."

"Is that why somebody took a shot at me after I got back? To keep me from tellin' about that mine?"

"Somebody shot at you? I don't know . . . I don't know about that."

"Uh-huh. They wanted plenty of time to go back there and stake their claims."

"Yes. That's what Dudley said." She fell silent again, then looked up. "Did you say they killed that Mr. Harvey?"

"They sure as hell did. Shot him down the way they tried to shoot me. There's a witness. Your lover boy and his sidekick are wanted for murder."

A sob came from her. "Oh my. I didn't mean for . . . this isn't what I . . ." Her shoulders shook as she sobbed silently.

"And I've got more news for you. It was all for nothin'."

"What?" Wiping her eyes with the palms of her

hands, she blinked at him. "What do you mean?"

Chuckling now, Buck said, "All that work they did trailin' us, all that blastin', grubbin', livin' like a bunch of coyotes, it was all for nothin'. If they weren't in trouble with the law, your lover boy would be comin' after you and he wouldn't be after your body. He'd be after your hide. He'd blame you for everything."

"I don't understand."

"That minin' claim you got, you better sell it fast, 'cause when the word gets out, you won't be able to give it away."

Puzzled blue eyes were fixed on him again. "I still don't understand."

Buck turned, went to the window, looked down on the street. His right hip ached and he wished he could sit down. There was no chair in the room, and he didn't want to sit on the bed beside her. Facing her again, thumbs hooked in his gunbelt, he said, "I should have known. It was there to see, but I was too damned dumb."

"What, Mr. Innes?"

"The mine. There wasn't a tool of any kind there. Nothin' but an empty box and some empty cans. If Spooky was workin' that mine he'd of left some tools there. Instead of packin' out his tools he'd of packed out all the rich rocks he could. Hell, he gave up on that mine over a year ago."

"What are you saying?"

"It's worthless. The rocks Spooky took out of there wasn't worth packin' to the mill." Another chuckle came from Buck, a dry one. "Old Spooky wasn't the expert gold hunter he thought he was."

"But, but you followed his tracks there."

No longer chuckling, Buck said, "Yeah, I did. The last few miles his track was plain as day. What happened is, Spooky knew a lot of men were tryin' to follow him to his mine, and he led 'em all around the mulberry bush just to make 'em work. But sometime this summer he decided he'd played the game long enough and he left sign for anybody that came along to see."

"But . . ."

He interrupted, "I didn't know where his mine was and I hunted over a lot of country before I run across his tracks. If I hadn't a gone north, I'd a cut his sign a lot sooner."

"The mine, you say it's worthless? Why do you say that?"

"You noticed that pile of rocks next to his cabin door? Well, there's another pile of rocks just like it out there east of the canyon. What I figure is this: Spooky blasted and hacked out some ore, what he thought was rich ore, and started to town with two burro loads. Only one of his burros went lame or got sick or somethin' and he had to leave some of the ore behind."

"So?"

"When he got home, he unloaded the other jack-ass by his cabin door and took some of the rocks, what he could carry hisself, to the assayer," Buck shook his head sadly. "Old Spooky must of been some disappointed. He was so disappointed he left them rocks right where he unloaded 'em."

The girl's shoulders slumped. "So my father didn't have a valuable gold mine." Then she straightened her shoulders, stood and faced Buck squarely. "If that's so, where did he get all that rich gold ore he brought to town? Tell me that, Mr. Innes."

A wry grin crossed Buck's face. "Ever hear of highgradin'?"

"What? What's that?"

"Highgradin'. It's what most of these miners do to help feed their families. When they get to blastin', hackin' and muckin' in the mines they sometimes come across some real rich stuff, and they put a few pieces in their pockets or in their lunch buckets or someplace. It adds another dollar a day to their sorry wages. That is, when they can get by with it."

"Do you mean they steal from their employers?"

"Yeah, only they don't think it's stealin'. It ain't agin' the law. A judge done ruled that gold ore is real estate and you can't steal real estate. It ain't a sin. They put gold ore in the collection plate at church, and the preachers are glad to get it. But . . ." Buck looked at the floor and scratched the stubble on his jaw. ". . . they can't buy groceries with it and the bartenders are afraid to touch it. They got to find a way to turn it into cash money."

He paused a moment, thinking. "There was an assayer in town that bought it from 'em and squeezed or cooked the gold out of it. But the mine owners got wise and run him off. They hired some thugs to beat up the miners that got caught highgradin'."

Pausing again, he saw that the girl was wide-eyed, waiting for him to go on. He swallowed and went on:

"That's when old Spooky got an idee. He met them miners out by the cemetery at night and collected the rich rocks from 'em. He stayed out of sight somewhere 'till he collected two burro loads. Then he packed it to the mill and told everybody he took it out of a rich vein he found. He split the money with the miners, prob'ly fifty-fifty." Another chuckle came from Buck. "Huh. No wonder he came and went in the dark and wouldn't tell anybody where his mine was."

Shoulders slumped again, Miss Hallows said, "So

my father was a fence for gold thieves."

"Yup. A fence or whatever you city folks call it. But I'll tell you somethin', he made enough money that way to keep on sendin' you some cash every month. And I'll bet you and your lover boy wasted no time spendin' it."

"Mr. White is my fiance."

"He's a thief and a killer."

For a second her head was up and her blue eyes flashed. "He . . ." Her head dropped again.

Buck walked to the window, looked down, walked back to face her. "I don't know what to think about you, Miss Hallows. You got mixed up with some hardcase cutthroats, and you sure ain't the most honest woman in the world. You fooled me and used me and almost got me killed. I wouldn't trust you any farther than I can throw you up the side of Signal Mountain. If you wasn't Spooky Hallows's daughter I'd try to get you arrested for somethin'."

She was wringing her hands now, looking to be on the verge of tears. "I . . . I'm sorry. I was a fool. I really didn't mean anyone any harm."

"All right, all right." Buck walked to the window and back, looking down at his boots. "All right. Tell you what. If you'll go see your dad, be nice to him and not take any more money from him, I won't tell him about this."

"What?" She was staring, open-mouthed. She sputtered, and gasped, "See him? Is he alive?"

"Yep," Buck said. "I believe he's alive and I believe I know where he is."

Buck Innes didn't take time to go to Mrs. Davenport's boarding house to shave or change clothes. He was planning to, but just as he got down to the hotel lobby the stage pulled up with a rattling of trace chains and a loud "Whoa." Wanting to get the day over, he quickly bought a ticket and was the last of six passengers to get aboard. He had to share a seat with a ragged miner and a well-dressed drummer. The drummer gave Buck a good looking over, eyeing his beard and dirty clothes. His expression showed he would rather sit on the facing seat with a woman and her two children.

"Mama," said a boy of about four, "why is that man over there sitting so funny?" The boy wore knickers and black stockings. Sun-bleached hair stuck out from under his bill cap. His shoes were laced up over his ankles.

"Hush," the woman said.

The man he was referring to was Buck Innes. Buck's right hip was a steady ache now, and he leaned as far to the left as he could, trying to ease the pain. The drummer leaned as far away from Buck as he could.

When the stage stopped at the Welty Ranch on Four Mile Creek to change horses, Buck got out and limped back and forth beside it until the ache eased somewhat. He didn't get back inside until he had to. Meanwhile the drummer had managed to switch sides, and Buck was now leaning toward the miner. The laboring man didn't seem to mind. "Kinda tiresome, ain't it," he said. "Yeah," Buck said. Soon the ache returned, and Buck's face screwed up.

"Mama," the boy said, "there's something wrong with that man."

"Hush."

The boy's eyes were wide, but he said no more. Buck tried to keep his face straight.

It was eighteen miles to Florissant, and by changing horses once it took only a little over two hours to get there. The stage pulled up in front of a white building with good lumber siding and a false front.

When Buck climbed sorely, slowly out of the coach he had to stand and lean against one of the big wheels for a few minutes. As he stood, he looked over the town.

Florissant was a smaller but older town than Cripple Creek, and the Colorado Midland Railroad had reached there years ago. From where Buck stood he could see the railroad yards, a busy place. Two big steam engines stood there, smoking and hissing, ready to help smaller engines pull rail cars up the grade east to the settlement named Divide or west to Leadville. It was a busy town with its railroad yard and sawmills. Lumber was stacked in high piles near the railroad, ready to be loaded onto flatbed cars and hauled east to Colorado City and Colorado Springs. Much of it went north from there to Denver and south to Pueblo. Lumber wagons pulled by four-horse teams creaked and groaned on the streets.

Though the town was busy there was none of the excitement that filled the air in Cripple Creek. Men on the streets all wore working men's clothes, and the women wore plain cotton dresses with few frills. Children played in the streets. Two young boys and two girls were rolling an iron wagon tire down the main street. Two other boys were riding bicycles. They rode unsteadily, and barely got out of the way of a lumber wagon. No one yelled at them. Here, people went about their business in a placid manner.

Buck carefully put all his weight on his right leg, and was surprised to find the leg held him up. He took a few tentative steps. The old ache subsided a little. Limping, he turned toward Castello's Mercantile.

The store was easy to find. A big sign over the door identified it as Castello's General Merchandise. In smaller letters at the bottom were the words,

"Country Produce Taken in Exchange for Goods."
Buck limped up onto the porch, opened a squeaky
screen door and went in. The store hadn't changed
since Buck had been there last, a couple of years
ago. Long glass showcases lined each side of the
room with walking space between them and rows of
shelves on the walls. The cases were filled with sew-
ing materials, cigars, candy and even rifle and pistol
ammunition. And yeah, there were the tailor-made
cigarettes that Spooky liked. Shelves behind the
cases held groceries of all kinds, including the hermetically sealed canned goods.

"Buck Innes, as I live and breathe." Mister Castello hurried up from the back of the store to shake
Buck's hand. "Haven't seen you since Old Yip was a
pup. Heard you made a hero of yourself down to
Canon City awhile back. How are you, anyway? You
look kind of peak-ud."

"I'm fine, John. A little worse for wear, but fine."

"Heard you sold your homesteads and stock.
What are you doing these days? Staying out of trouble?"

Buck had to grin. "Trouble's my name. But, yeah,
I ain't wanted by the law or anything."

"Did you come in on the stage? You look tired.
Want to sit down? Come on back in my office."

"Naw. I'm, uh, I'm lookin' for somebody. You
know Andy Hallows? Old Spooky, we call him now-
adays. Seen him lately?"

Suddenly, the genial expression on the merchant's
face changed to one of worry. "Well, uh . . ."

"All right," Buck said, still wearing a weak grin.
"Tell me this much, do you know a gent name of
Shoemaker?"

"There's two Shoemakers. They're brothers. One is
an off-bearer at the sawmill. The other works out at

216

the OxBow Ranch. Which one are you looking for?"

"The one that lives here in town, I reckon."

"Oh, he's easy to find. He's on the early morning shift, and he ought to be getting off work about now. Go down south two blocks and turn west to the next street. He lives in a one-room clapboard shack with a tarpaper roof."

"Obliged, John. If you see Spooky, er Andy, tell him I'm lookin' for him. He's got nothin' to fear from me and he knows it."

"I will, Buck."

Following the storekeeper's directions, Buck found the shack. It was obviously a bachelor's den without curtains on the windows or flowers in the yard. The windows hadn't been washed lately. Only a dirt path led to the shack from the street. Buck limped up to the door and yelled, "Hello. Hello inside."

No answer.

Maybe he wasn't going about it right. Town folks didn't holler, they knocked on doors. Buck knocked. Waited. Knocked again.

Aw hell. He couldn't decide whether to wait or go back to the store and buy a tin of sardines and some soda crackers and eat. He could come back later. Shoemaker ought to be at home by then. His growling stomach decided for him.

He started down the path back to the street when he saw a man walking up the street in his direction. The man fit the description. And sure enough, he turned onto the path.

"Are you Shoemaker?" Buck asked when the man was close.

"That I am. Who are you?" His voice was pleasant enough.

"My name is Buck Innes. I'm lookin' for somebody. I'm lookin' for Andy Hallows."

Shoemaker stood ten feet away from Buck and looked him over carefully, eyed the sixgun on his hip. "You from Cripple Creek?"

"Yeah, I am, but . . ."

"I don't know no Andy Hallows."

"Listen," Buck said, "I don't represent no law and I don't work for no mine owners. Andy and me, we're long-time friends. We go way back before Cripple Creek was born. Some folks are worried about him. His daughter is worried about him."

"His daughter? Is she still around?"

"Naw. She went back to Denver, but I told her I'd try to find her dad."

"Mister, are you lyin' to me?"

"No sir," Buck said. "I wouldn't harm a hair on Andy's head."

Shoemaker's eyes bored into Buck's. Finally, he looked down, back at Buck, then to his left. "See that house over there, the one that was painted brown?"

Again, Buck knocked on a door. Waited. Knocked. He heard footsteps. Breathing shallow breaths now, Buck waited and wondered. Was it really Spooky Hallows coming to the door? The door opened.

The man who stood in the doorway had a wild gray beard and gray hair sticking up in all directions. He was a small man, wrinkled and wiry. His mouth dropped open and he stared.

Buck said, "Andy, you are one hard son-of-a-gun to find. You still alive?"

Stammering, the bearded man said, "B—Buck Innes. You old coyote. What in the name of sin are you doin' here?"

"Lookin' for you, Andy. Some folks think you're dead. Your daughter's worried about you."

Andy — Spooky — Hallows looked past Buck, looked in all directions, then stepped back. "Buck. Come in here. Haul your old carcass inside this house."

"Nobody followed me, Andy. Nobody in Cripple Creek knows where you are." Buck entered the one-room house. Another bachelor's house. A narrow cot on the far side had a tarp for a cover instead of a quilt. The two-lid cookstove in the corner had a smoke-blackened pot on one lid and a coffee pot on the other. Canned food, a sack of flour and a sack of coffee stood on a wooden shelf near the stove. Firewood was stacked inside a wooden crate against a wall.

"Come in and set," Spooky Hallows said. "Set here at the table. I'll light a fire and make some coffee. Have you et lately?"

"Not since early this mornin'." Buck pulled a wooden chair away from a small plank table and sat. "Got anything to eat in here?"

"I got ever'thing, Buck. Eggs, ham, some good bread. Even some butter. How 'bout some eggs and smoke-cured ham?"

"I could eat the seams out of a whore's drawers."

With a dry chuckle, the bearded man went about building a fire in the cookstove. He got a flame going, then sat across the table from Buck. "Won't take long to heat a skillet, and we'll eat." He was silent a moment, then said, "Annie, my daughter, was here lookin' for me, but I didn't know it 'till after she left. I told ever'body to keep mum about me. That's why she didn't find me."

"I figured as much."

"Did you see her, Buck? What does she look like?"

"She's a damned fine lookin' young woman. Knows how to be a lady. Purty as a pup." It wasn't the whole truth, but it wasn't a lie either. "She looks a lot like her mother, the way I remember her mother lookin', and she looks like you too." Buck grinned. "She's got the best of both."

They were silent again, each trying to think of the right words. The fire crackled.

"Andy, I know about your mine and I know what you was doin'."

"Oh." The pale blue eyes in the wrinkled face grew sad. "Does my daughter know?"

Buck managed to avoid an outright lie. "I . . . uh, she went back to Denver when she couldn't find you."

"That's what Bob Shoemaker found out. When I heard a young lady was lookin' for me I figured it was her and I sent Bob to Cripple Creek to tell her where I was."

"Yeah. I heard somebody named Shoemaker was lookin' for her and later I heard he was from here."

"That's how you knew where to find me."

"Yeah."

Silence. Then, "I had to get out of there, Buck."

"I figured you did. They busted some heads. You took 'em for more than anybody else did. They'd of killed you."

"I'm goin' back some day. I still got some property there."

"No hurry about it. The way that town's growin' your few acres're gonna be worth somethin' one a these days. How you doin' here?"

"Purty good. I realized enough profit while it lasted to keep me a long time. Prob'ly 'till I die. It don't cost much to live around here."

"Nobody knows where you are but me. I guessed

you was here, but I didn't tell nobody. Why don't you write to your daughter and tell her. Maybe she'll come back to see you."

"I'll do it. I, uh, I quit sendin' her money. I swore once to send her money ever' month 'till she was twenty-five or got married or somethin'. She was twenty-five last April eight. Did she say if she was married yet?"

"She didn't say, and I didn't ask." Another half-truth.

"She looked good, you say? Healthy and ever'thing?"

"She's fine, Andy."

The bearded man got up, sliced some ham and tossed it into a hot skillet. He broke some eggs and fried them on top of the ham. When they were done, he slid them off the skillet onto two tin plates. They ate, drank coffee, leaned back in their chairs. Andy Hallows lit one of his cigarettes. He asked, "You still livin' at Mrs. Davenport's boardin' house?"

"Yup. I've got a soft bed there, and that woman sure can cook."

"You got a place to bunk tonight?"

"I'm goin' back. I hear Old Hundley runs a stage down that road several times a day and the next one's a couple hours before sundown."

"Yep. He's makin' money while he can. He's afraid the railroad's gonna put him out of business."

"Prob'ly will, but not this year."

Before he left, Buck asked, "Need anything, Andy? Money? Some chuck or anything?"

"Naw. Like I said, I've got enough stashed away to last me a long time."

"Well . . ." Buck didn't know how to say goodbye.

"Think she'll come to see me, my daughter?"

"She came once, didn't she?"

221

"I'll shave and keep my clothes clean in case she does."

"Adios, Andy."

"So long, Buck. See you sometime."

It had been a long day, and it was a long ride back to Cripple Creek. A man in business clothes wanted to make conversation, but Buck didn't feel like talking. The stage stopped at the top of the volcanic rim as usual, then the teamster cracked his long whip and hollered, "Heeyah."

Down the hill they went, horses on a dead run, coach bouncing and swaying, passengers hanging onto anything they could find, hanging onto each other. Pedestrians saw it coming, hurried out of the way, stopped and watched. And finally, "Who-o-oa, who-o-oa now."

Buck Innes was as tired as he was when he'd walked back from Shotgun Canyon. He was so tired he could barely make it up the path to the boarding house. It was nearly dark, and he knew he was too late for supper, but he also knew Mrs. Davenport would find something for him to eat if he asked her to. He wasn't hungry.

On his way he started singing under his breath, "Oh, the Camp Town . . ." Then he said aloud, "Aw, shut up, Buck Innes. You hate that song. You know you do."

Finally, he was there.

Hadigan was sitting on the porch, picking his teeth with a wooden toothpick. He watched Buck approach without saying anything. Not until Buck had climbed the steps, plopped down with a long sigh into his favorite chair and lifted his boots to the porch rail, did he speak.

"Buck, where in hell you been this time?"

"Aw, nowhere."

"What've you been doin'?"

"Nothin'."